Possessed of a   Miss
Cassandra Wells is returning to Society after a few years'
absence as chaperone of her harum-scarum niece, Susan.
It is unfortunate indeed that the very first person Cassandra meets is Jonathan, Lord Verax, whose offer she had
spurned in her debutante days. Will he take her at her
word and pay court to the lovely Susan, or does his mocking manner and rapier-sharp tongue conceal traces of his
old love? The duelling between Cassandra and Verax
reaches such a pitch that only the Prince Regent himself
can resolve the struggle.

Duel of Love

Helen May

MILLS & BOON LIMITED
London · Sydney · Toronto

First published in Great Britain 1980
by Mills & Boon Limited, 17–19 Foley Street,
London W1A 1DR

© Helen May 1980
Australian copyright 1980
Philippine copyright 1980

ISBN 0 263 73225 8

Filmset in 11 on 12½pt Plantin

Made and printed in Great Britain by
C. Nicholls & Company Ltd
The Philips Park Press, Manchester

CHAPTER
ONE

MISS CASSANDRA WELLS stirred in her peaceful slumber, then opened her eyes, wondering what had disturbed her. Moonlight slanted across her half-tester bed and gave the snowy drapes a blue glow. She listened carefully to the sounds which reached her on the frosty air, before sighing and climbing out of bed. Her fire had burned low, and she shivered and turned the face of her gilded clock to catch the light.

It was half-past one, and she reached for her warm wrapper and crossed her large bedroom to the window.

Opening her casement with care, she looked out into the garden and gave a second deep sigh. A ladder leaned upon the sill of the room next to hers, clutched at its base by a man dressed in a long, caped coat, boots, and a beaver hat.

The voice which hissed directions to him from the window held all the irritation of a young lady about to elope with a man who showed reluctance to pursue what he evidently considered an unreasoned course of action.

Cassandra's niece, Miss Susan Wells, leaned further into the night and her nut-brown curls gleamed in the moonlight. "Hugh, for pity's sake!

How do you suppose I am to climb on to a ladder without assistance?"

Hugh's tones had reached almost a desperate pitch. "If I do not hold the ladder it will slip. There is no purchase upon these icy flagstones; certainly not enough to trust the weights of us both. Cannot you call your maid to help?"

"Bella will go straight to my aunt. She is as stick-in-the-mud as my Aunt Cassandra's maid. You *must* climb the ladder!"

"And I tell you it is not safe. Susan, will you please go to the front door like any sensible female? This is ludicrous!"

"Ludicrous?"

Cassandra was interested to note how much vehemence could be injected into one whispered word.

"Ludicrous, is it? Very well! I will climb down myself, but I shall hold you responsible if I break my neck or something."

Sensing the reckless determination in her niece's tone, Cassandra left the window and slipped her feet into a pair of pumps, before pulling an Indian cashmere shawl about her shoulders and opening her door. She was unsurprised to see two other doors open almost simultaneously with hers and two figures appear.

Nurse wore a man's dressing gown and a nightcap of astonishing proportions and Eliza, her maid, had swathed her face in flannel against an attack of the neuralgia.

"That hoyden!" exploded Nurse with all the liberty of an Ancient Retainer. "She's off again!"

"Miss Susan Wells," remarked Eliza, her tones more than usually prim in an implied reproof for her colleague's familiarity, "does indeed seem to be indulging in another distressing prank."

Both women had kept their voices low, and when Cassandra opened the door of her niece's bedchamber Susan's shriek of alarm was real. "Oh! Aunt Cassandra, is it you? Was ever a girl plagued so before? Others seem to manage the most romantic of escapades while I . . ." Here she broke off to call down. "Hugh, you have left it too long and now we are undone! My aunt has discovered us!"

Cassandra walked to the window and looked down into the anguished face of Hugh Egerton, son of the local rector. "You will come to my drawing-room, Hugh," she commanded coldly. "We have matters to discuss."

She closed the casement with a bang and turned to regard her niece by the light of candles which Eliza had ignited, while Nurse hurried to draw the bolts on the front door to admit Hugh.

"You had much better return to bed, Susan. We will talk in the morning."

"But if you are going to speak to Hugh, I should be present. This is also my affair!"

"It most certainly is 'your affair', as you term it. I would not have believed you could so persuade a man destined for the church."

"Oh, it *is* my fault!" exclaimed Susan. "He did not at all want to elope, but we love one another so desperately and no one will allow us to marry for years, and I . . . I said I would not regard his suit with favour if he did not consent to run away with me."

At Cassandra's look she stared at the floor and toyed with the fringe of her shawl. "Hugh wishes to become ordained before we wed. He says he must be in a position to offer me a home – however humble, for as you know, his papa is not rich, and there are all the other children, but I love him so. . . ."

She stopped to draw breath and tears spilled from her hazel eyes and rolled over the soft, rosy curves of her sixteen-year-old cheeks. Cassandra was fascinated.

"Can you weep whenever you wish? I understand from your Aunt Elizabeth Yorke that you shed tears when you were prised from an attachment to the youngest son of a baronet only three months ago, and that your tears flowed copiously at your board school when the distraught headmistress separated you from the poverty-stricken French refugee nobleman who instructed you in dancing. You appear to have a positive passion for becoming entangled with unsuitable lovers!"

Susan flinched. "I cannot cry at will. Can I help it if I have too much sensibility?" She twisted the ribbons of her gown. "I do love Hugh, you know. This is different from the others."

Cassandra hesitated. "Well, at least we know him to be a man of honour – in spite of the events of tonight – and you have been acquainted with him these many years. You may descend with me to see Master Hugh."

"He's waiting in the small drawing-room," announced Nurse, before she and Eliza ranged themselves behind their mistress and the four entered the room to confront the appalled young man.

"So there you are," said Nurse. "Young whippersnapper! In my day you would have been flogged out of the grounds by footmen. Pity times have changed."

"That will do," said Cassandra. "I will speak to him. There is no need for you and Eliza to remain longer out of your beds."

"I will await you in your bedchamber," declared Eliza. "No one can say that I fail in my estimation in what is proper to you."

Nurse touched her large cap with hands which shook theatrically. "I feel as if I might be about to begin a headache," she announced, "but you, poor, dear Mrs. Cole, are in a worse state with your neuralgia. I will find you a soothing draught for it."

"You are too generous, Mrs. Webster," replied Eliza, "when I am sure you must be exhausted."

The two elderly women left, and in spite of the gravity of the situation Cassandra was forced to turn her head to hide her quivering lips as Susan remarked, "Now they are calling one another 'Mrs.'. Tomorrow they will be ranged against us both."

Hugh had not uttered a word, but when Cassandra turned to him she felt pity for his haggard white face as he said with a bow, "There are no words in which to express my regret, Miss Wells. Of course, you must see Papa tomorrow." A spasm crossed his face, for he loved and respected his parents and, until tonight, had been a model son.

"Oh, must you?" cried Susan. "It is all my fault. Hugh did not want to elope – I explained. . . ."

"Be silent, Susan!" ordered Hugh in a voice which made Susan gape and raised Cassandra's brows. "Of course your aunt's duty is to speak to Papa!"

"Is that how you feel you must repay all his devotion and sacrifices, Hugh? For they do make a most tremendous effort to keep you at Oxford. How could you have helped your brothers and sisters by such an example? How can you have contemplated such an escapade?"

Hugh ran a hand through his fair hair, which stood in spikes, and a stricken look came into his grey eyes. "Nothing you say can make me feel more wretched that I already do! Papa will be so hurt – and as for Mama. . . ." His voice broke, and if he had not been a man of eighteen years Cassandra thought he might have wept.

She decided he had been punished enough. "Listen carefully, Hugh. To inform your parents of what has happened would relieve you of a great part of the burden of guilt and lay it upon them. That would be cruel indeed, for I know that you are a good son and will not forget the lesson you have learned. If you will promise me to return to Oxford as secretly as you must have left and work for your ordination, I swear that not a word of this will reach your family's ears."

Hugh stared at her, a mixture of emotions crossing his boyish face, before he followed a bow to Susan by one to Cassandra. "I hope you will allow me to pay my addresses to Susan when I am in a proper position to think of marriage."

Cassandra nodded noncommittally, then a thought struck her. "Hugh, I cannot help knowing that you have limited funds, and Susan always spends her pin-money as soon as she receives it. Just how did you plan to run away together?"

Hugh grimaced. "I . . . I borrowed Mama's little gig. I could not take Papa's, for he must have it for his round of parishioners."

"And harnessed to it?" pursued Cassandra.

Colour ran up under the fair skin. "Mama's carriage pony."

Cassandra and he stared at one another for a moment, both held by the vision of the lovers journeying from Somerset in search of a parson to marry them, seated in a hooded gig drawn by an ancient, fat horse who had not travelled faster than a walk for years. Then Hugh bowed again and was gone.

Susan threw herself into an upholstered chair and covered her face. "I cannot bear it! My heart will break – I know it will!"

Cassandra pulled her shawl about her and walked to the fireplace to gain the advantage of the still-warm coals. Her hands trembled in her effort to control a sudden longing to seize Susan by the shoulders and shake her until her small, flawless teeth rattled.

Susan, discovering that her histrionics were not bringing the desired result, sat up straight. "Say something, please, Aunt Cassandra. Punish me how you will – I deserve it!"

Cassandra turned to face her niece. "You seem to treat life as a stage entertainment. Punishment and talking have no effect upon you. No, I shall pursue the matter differently. Your behaviour has so far given your poor mama small cause for happiness."

"You will not tell her!" Susan was genuinely alarmed.

"I must suppose you to care for her, then."

"How can you say so? She is my mother!"

"And far from robust."

"Oh, Mama is a sad invalid! I am sure I do not know why my family conspire to keep me so often from her side."

"Do you not, indeed? Well, you will have time to reflect. You will go now to your room and remain until I send for you."

Something in her aunt's clear blue eyes deterred Susan from arguing, and she left. Cassandra entered her bedchamber to find Nurse sitting so rigidly upright that she might have been wearing one of the backboards she had once used on her charges. She eyed Cassandra with disfavour.

"I took the liberty of persuading poor Mrs. Cole to retire. I will assist you, Miss Cassandra."

"Very well, Nurse, you may help me off with my wrapper."

Swallowing her disappointment at her mistress's meek reaction, Nurse folded the shawl and laid out the wrapper with hands twisted with rheumatics and Cassandra felt an upsurge of devotion towards the woman who had lived her life for The Family and had been mother and friend to her since the early demise of her mama.

"I do not know how I should go on without you and Eliza to care for me, dear Nurse. You are my family."

Nurse coughed to conceal emotion. "'Tis a pity you cannot rid yourself of that *naughty* child. Some strong man should marry her."

"Her life has not been easy," Cassandra pointed out gently. "My brother doted on her, and his death left her deeply sad. And she seldom sees her mama."

"And whose fault is that?"

"We should not apportion blame. My sister-in-law is insistent that Susan should not be worried by the gravity of her heart condition. The girl lacks an anchor."

When Nurse had blown out the candle and left Cassandra once more in the blue stillness, she lay thinking deeply. Her sister Elizabeth Yorke had sent Susan to her when advised by her physicians that she must rest completely during her pregnancy. Her eighth, reflected Cassandra, her mouth grimacing a little. Her sister claimed to be content, but Cassandra failed to comprehend her assertion when she watched her sister, her figure grown flabby, her day-to-day existence one long round of managing her household with limited means.

Nevertheless, it seemed that Susan was only too irritatingly anxious to enter the subservient state of matrimony, though the fortune left her by her grandparents on her mother's side would always see her comfortable. That is, thought Cassandra, if it were not squandered by the wrong kind of husband!

She was still in thought as she fell asleep and awoke as Eliza entered with her tea and bread and butter. She assured her mistress that her neuralgia was quite cured, and the asperity of her tones indicated that the daily battle with Nurse would once more be joined.

Cassandra followed a resolution to write to Susan's mother, and during the days which followed refused to discuss with her niece anything pertaining to the attempted elopement. As soon as the reply arrived she sent for Susan, who perched herself on the edge of a satin-covered sofa and regarded her aunt with limpid eyes. Her look of girlish innocence both intrigued and worried her aunt. It was not assumed and could, Cassandra feared, lead Susan into the most dangerous of situations which would preclude any future happiness.

"I have heard from your mama," began Cassandra and held up a white hand at Susan's horrified gasp. "No, I have not burdened her with your misdemeanour, but I have her agreement to follow a certain course. I can tell you now that I have her permission to introduce you into society – to make your Come-out, in fact – at a ridiculously early age. You will not reach seventeen until late Spring but, in my opinion, the sooner you are safely betrothed to a trustworthy man of substance, the sooner the whole family may return to its peaceful existence."

"M . . . make my Come-out! I thought I was to be punished!" A puzzled look puckered her face. "But why should I not then have married Hugh?"

"You seem to understand nothing! Hugh knows he could never support you in your proper state in life, even if you do not. Oh, I realise he has grand dreams where he may be transported to some rich living, but without family wealth or patronage that is not likely to happen."

"I would still love him!"

Cassandra smote one hand in the other. "Susan! You would humiliate him! It is clear to me, though not it seems to you, that he feels his lesser position most keenly! You are as fit to assume the responsibility of a poor parson's wife as . . . as the babe carried by your Aunt Elizabeth! I would not dream of pressing you into an unwelcome union, but you must be given the opportunity of meeting with men of wealth and breeding to match your own. I have not the least doubt that all memory of Hugh will fade from your mind."

Many expressions flitted across Susan's pretty countenance as she tried to encompass dismay and delight at the same time. Delight won, and she beamed. "I will be good," she promised. "Oh, how can I wait? It is an age before the London Season."

"You will not have to be patient quite so long. We shall go first to a watering place where we shall find a little lively amusement, and where I may observe your conduct. Not for worlds will I take you to London if I cannot rely upon your not antagonising the hostesses upon whom your success will depend."

"Oh, I shall be well behaved," breathed Susan. "How very fortunate that Bath is so near and we shall not be handicapped by the weather! Shall you take lodgings there? Shall we buy gowns – or wait for London? How exciting it will be – The Assemblies – The Pump Rooms – The Libraries . . ."

"We are not going to Bath," interrupted Cassandra, and stared firmly over the open-mouthed Susan's head. "As you may know, I was born in Clifton, near Bristol, which is also the site of the Hot Wells. It is a delightful village, where I shall be certain of meeting some of my friends, and will be inhabited by quite a number of folk taking the waters."

"But surely . . . Bath is so much more fashionable – so much gayer – oh, please, Aunt . . ."

Cassandra said coldly, "Is this the way you fulfil your promise? Already I question my decision."

Susan ran to her aunt and clung to her hand. "I beg your pardon most humbly. Of course, we will go anywhere you say. Clifton it shall be, and I know it will be delightful."

Cassandra hoped that Susan was right. Only Elizabeth had guessed at the disturbing images

which her birthplace aroused in her mind, and only
she could suspect the truth of Cassandra's refusal to
go to Bath.

Clifton held many sad memories, in spite of her
praise of it to Susan, and she had not been back since
her father's death, four years before, when the family
home had been sold and the proceeds divided between herself and her surviving brother and sister.
She thought with pain of the death of her mother,
worn out by bearing too many babies. She remembered the difficult years of housekeeping for a man
who had been barely on speaking terms with his
other offspring. Marriage, it had seemed to Cassandra from an early age, came unavoidably accompanied by male domination, children and confusion
and suffering, and a lack of opportunity for a woman
to pursue any activity associated with an independent mind, and she was thankful that at the age of
twenty-six she was safe from matchmakers.

She stared from the window into the frost-laden
garden, where every day her servants placed food for
the birds hard put to survive in this terrible January
of 1814. Susan left to take stock of her wardrobe, and
Cassandra lost herself in thoughts of yesterday's call
upon Elizabeth.

Her sister had been cheerful, though Cassandra
could not truly believe that any woman could find joy
in her predicament, and had listened intently to
Cassandra's account of Susan's misbehaviour.

"You are a martyr to consider a return to London," she commented, her eyes fixed firmly on a
baby's cap she was stitching. "I recall when you left –
was it three years ago? – you declared it to be trivial
and tedious." She carefully snipped a thread. "By

the way, have you heard of the return to England of Lord Verax – Captain Ashford that was?"

Cassandra shrugged. "Why should that interest me? I know, of course, of the unexpected demise of his relative which raised him to the nobility, but I am sure our little friendship has long been forgotten. It has by me, anyway."

"*Little friendship?* He loved you!"

"He was a callow youth of nineteen and I but seventeen when he offered marriage. I can see him now – thin, red with emotion . . ."

"You made him nervous!"

"Must we speak of him? I am not permitted to argue with you in your delicate state," smiled Cassandra.

"Very well, but when you mention taking Susan to a watering-place I wonder if you know that Verax has been ordered to take the waters."

Cassandra walked to the fireplace and leaned on the mantel, staring into the fire. "That could scarcely interest me." Her voice was muffled as she continued, "I know he was wounded."

"Then you may have heard that Lord Wellington's surgeons could not reach the musket-ball in his shoulder – he suffered much. . . ." A strangled sound from her sister made Elizabeth pause, then she went on. "He was sent to England where Sir Everard Home finally extracted the ball, but not until inflammation of the lung had set in. He recovered, but now must visit a watering-place. I hear he is quite the man of fashion, so he will probably choose Bath."

Cassandra turned, her face flushed beneath her crown of deep gold hair. "I am not perturbed by the idea of meeting Jonathan Verax," she said coolly.

But just as she was leaving, she remarked in a casual manner that she believed she would take Susan to Clifton.

CHAPTER
TWO

THE journey to Clifton, where Cassandra had written for apartments for herself and her companions, though short in miles, proved to be trying. The horses and carriages slipped and jolted over the frozen, rutted roads and there were times during the ascent of the steep Bristol hills when Cassandra feared they would slide backwards into the River Avon. But they arrived without mishap, to be greeted warmly by the hotel proprietor and conducted to spacious apartments.

Susan looked about her, amazed. "It is all beautiful! I did not know hotels were like this."

"The Clifton Hotel is quite different from the general run, and it is perfectly proper for us to take accommodation here. It is connected with the Assembly Rooms and houses places for cards, billiards and for eating – and all manner of recreation. We shall have plenty of amusements without needing to brave the cold."

"What an angel you are!" Susan launched herself at her aunt and planted a resounding kiss on her cheek.

Cassandra enjoyed the feeling of popularity, but took the opportunity, while Nurse and the maids unpacked, to give her charge some words of warning. "Susan, although I do not think your youthful waywardness will have reached the ears of the powerful leaders of fashion, I cannot too strongly impress upon you the need for decorum. Only let one hint of hoydenish or immodest behaviour come to the attention of the Lady Patronesses of Almacks, and your career as a lady of fashion will come to a sad end. When I think of the set-downs given by Madame de Lieven – or Lady Castlereagh and Mrs. Burrell . . ." Cassandra shuddered. "Lady Jersey's husband once declined to fight a duel with the excuse that if he fought all the persons whom his wife had offended by a *refusal* of a voucher, he would become a target for pistol practice."

Susan asked, "How does one manage to control admirers in London?"

"You must keep them at a distance with kind but firm words, referring them, if necessary, to me as your guardian and chaperone."

Susan gave her a sideways glance. "You are altogether too young and pretty to be my chaperone, Aunt Cassandra."

"Flattery has no effect upon me, Susan. Have I your promise to behave?"

"Oh, indeed you have. That is – I always mean to be good, but somehow I hate to hurt the feelings of the young men who are so marvellously satisfying in the way they describe my . . . my charms. It seems ungracious to repel them."

"Then you must learn to do it graciously. Believe me, Susan, it is the nature of a man to lay siege to any young female of beauty, especially one who also has a fortune. Man is a vain animal. He must feel always that we will greet his advances with pleasure and his purpose with sympathy. It is up to a woman to teach him his place."

"Is that what you did, Aunt Cassandra? Is that why you never married?"

"Susan, that is impertinent in the extreme!"

Susan took her aunt's hand. "Pray forgive me, dearest of aunts. I did not mean it so. But you are very handsome in appearance, and have also a considerable fortune from your godmother . . ." Her voice trailed away beneath the icy blue gaze turned upon her. "I will speak of it no more," she promised.

"See that you do not, Susan. You must learn to accept, as I have, that it is not my way to lose my heart – or head – over any man. And now may I suggest that you retire to your own bedchamber and rest, as I propose to do. Today is Tuesday, which is the evening on which a regular Ball is held."

Susan's eyes shone and her lips parted in a smile of pure joy. "A Ball! Oh, Aunt, you are the kindest of creatures."

As Cassandra lay near her fire upon a day-bed, covered by Nurse with a blanket, she found she could not induce her usual sense of composure, and again she deplored the necessity for looking after Susan.

Images from the past came to her mind. She and Jonathan had been childhood friends and she had come to regard him in a sisterly fashion, accepting carelessly his single-minded admiration for her while she learned to flirt discreetly with others.

His behaviour at a betrothal ball for a mutual friend had surprised and shocked her. He had accompanied her out on to a balcony, seeking relief from the hot atmosphere of the ballroom, and as they enjoyed the cool moonlight he had taken her hand and stammered out his love for her.

Amused, she had first accused him of imbibing wine too freely, but his denial had been vehement as he protested that his passion for her was the most important matter of his life.

Still she could not believe him.

"Come now, Jonathan," she laughed. "Admit that you are bewitched by the music, the beauty of the night."

She held up her white arms to the moon, and light glinted on the gold of her bracelets. The sight was too much for his control and he caught her about her slender waist, his lips seeking hers.

Her fury and his protestations had been interrupted by a languid voice and they had turned to see Sir Vincent Pierce, surrounded as always by giggling cronies who were assisting him to run through the fortune built by his careful father. Sir Vincent, only seven years older than Jonathan, but experienced in vice, held a quizzing glass to the scene.

"La, Jonathan," he drawled, "I think I must give you a lesson on how to court the fair sex. It is not done in the style of a bull charging at a gate, but rather as a matador, with cunning use of temptation."

Jonathan's eyes glittered with fury as he held out his arm to Cassandra. "Pray, allow me to escort you back to the ballroom, ma'am."

Sir Vincent moved forward. "Nay, Ashford, you have made a sorry hash! I am sure Miss Wells will honour me with her company. I am almost sure she has engaged herself to me for the next country dance."

Cassandra stirred again on her couch as she remembered. One slight movement on her part towards Jonathan, a quick rejoinder to turn aside Sir Vincent's malevolence, would have saved her friend from further humiliation. What had possessed her to turn from him and accept the arm proffered by the baronet?

Jonathan had not called upon her again, and the next news she received was that he had persuaded his soldier father to purchase an Ensigncy for him and he had accompanied his parent back to India.

Cassandra had wept secret tears, deploring her behaviour and regretting Jonathan's reaction which had rendered it impossible for her to retract words and actions which she had immediately recognised as unnecessarily wounding, and furthermore, reflected no credit upon her own demeanour and attitude to life.

Major Ashford had died in India and Jonathan had joined Wellington's army in the fight against Bonaparte, and had not set foot in England until he had been sent home in an urgent attempt to save his life.

He had never married, but she must suppose him to have long forgotten that early passion. Why had she returned to Clifton where memory was strong? The vexatious Susan could have waited until the London Season began!

She gave up trying to rest and thought of the dress she would wear that evening. She knew that her gowns were not of the latest mode, although adequate in her village of Ridgefield where she was the principal lady. She would buy new in town, and they would, naturally, be the conservative garments suitable for a chaperone.

Eyeing the half-dress of grey crape over white satin with its grey chenille trimming which Eliza had laid out, Cassandra told herself firmly that she was too old to mind that the years away from high society had outdated her wardrobe and put inches on her figure. Nevertheless, when she rose, she had reached the decision that, in spite of the prevalence of large ladies encouraged by the tastes of the royal princes, she would eat more sparingly in the hope that the London mantua-makers would exclaim once more over her fine, firm figure.

Susan was deliciously pretty in a white lace over-dress and a pale yellow satin slip, her hair crowned with a fashionable Wellington wreath of laurel in yellow and white foil. The two ladies descended to the ballroom at the correct hour of eight o'clock, to be greeted by Mr. William Pennington, wearing his medallion of office as Master of Ceremonies.

Susan was joyously regarded by all the young men without partners, and one whom Mr. Pennington considered suitable having been presented to her, she was soon tripping down the first country dance with light feet, her eyes shining with pleasure.

Cassandra seated herself on one of the chaperones' benches and made a stern effort to control feet which had apparently assumed a wayward rhythmic movement of their own. She talked with old friends – married now with increasing families – acting as chaperones to various nieces and wards – and parried questions and remarks from elderly ladies whose past acquaintance with her family gave them the notion that they were at liberty to enquire intimately into her state of non-marriage and the reason there-for. Then she sat thinking of the weary months which lay ahead when, with self-sacrificing fervour, she would feel impelled to attend any function at which Susan might meet an eligible husband. She could only hope that a betrothal would soon relieve her of some of the burden.

She did not immediately realise that Mr. Pennington seemed to be under the illusion that she was available for dancing. He had approached her, accompanying a tall figure and was stammering an introduction. His embarrassment revealed that he was aware of his social solecism, and Cassandra looked wonderingly at the insolent person who had made the Master of Ceremonies so far forget what was due to her. She went cold inside.

"You may safely leave us, Mr. Pennington," advised the tall man. "Miss Wells and I are friends from years past."

Cassandra held out a hand encased in a grey kid glove. "Captain Ashford," she began, then, feeling annoyance at her lapse, continued, "Lord Verax, I should say! I did not look to see you here."

Verax bent his head over her hand and his lips brushed her glove. "Nor I you. I understood that you had retired from society. It seems a pity to deprive London of your wit and charm, though I see there is at present a good reason for it."

Cassandra stared at him as his eyes travelled over her garb. Was he mocking her? She could not be sure. The awkward boy had turned into a man of self-possession.

"If you are referring to my attire, sir, I am not in any kind of mourning. I consider this . . . raiment . . . suitable for one who is chaperoning a young woman on her first venture into the fashionable world."

"You! A chaperone!"

Again she looked sharply into his face. He was still slender, but now it was with the whipcord thinness of a campaigning soldier. His features held lines of suffering and the brown skin failed to conceal underlying pallor which told of illness. His manner was one of experienced sophistication which overwhelmed her by its unexpectedness, and she sensed that beneath the impeccable cut of his blue velvet dress coat, with the elegant gilt buttons and French cuffs, his thin form contained athletic strength. His white cravat was knotted in expert style, and the height of his collar was a triumph of compromise between fashion and foolishness.

"Will you not ask me to be seated, Cassandra?"

"It will not be considered seemly for a gentleman to join a lady on the chaperones' benches!"

"How severe you have become! My memories of you . . ."

". . . are best forgotten, sir!"

He gave her a lazy smile. "Are they indeed? Well, will you join me in a turn about the room. Is that permitted? I would ask you to dance, but my medical advisers do not allow it."

"Oh! I am sorry, Jonathan! I heard how you have suffered. Are you feeling better?"

A shadow crossed his face. "I have improved a good deal, but I have been told that my campaigning days are past. It causes me great grief. I have loved the life of a soldier, even though my reason for enlisting was . . ."

For a moment he seemed to share her embarrassment, and there was a brief silence. He said gently, "I do not think, Cassandra, that the other chaperones will mind if I sit with you. Several of them have been favouring me with quite indulgent smiles."

He seated himself and crossed one grey-trousered leg over the other.

Her anger rose again. "Please go away. You are making me conspicuous!"

He gazed at her. "I swear you are more beautiful than ever. But what is that ridiculous contraption covering your lovely hair?"

"It is a cap, sir, as well you know."

To her fury and astonishment Verax's hand slid down the thin black ribbon of his eyeglass, through which he regarded her with exaggerated amazement. "So it is! I never thought to see you in something so . . . well, but naturally, a chaperone must wear a cap formidable enough to depress the pretensions of any unsuitable young man who might approach her charge."

Cassandra bit her lip. She had chosen the fabrication of lace with particular attention to its austerity. "I had not thought to see you in Clifton," she remarked, repeating herself in her confusion.

"Had you not? May I assume that if you had anticipated meeting me you would have worn something more attractive?"

The fact that he had read her mind correctly made Cassandra even more cross. "I would have expected your medical advisers to send you to Bath – where you could have exerted your charms on so many more ladies than you will find here."

"So! Do you find me charming now? On our last – unfortunate encounter you appeared to set Sir Vincent's value above mine – as he was swift to appreciate."

Without pausing for a reply he said, "If you thought I was in Bath and came here I must suppose, alas, that you are bent on avoiding me. But you see, Cassandra, I am here and we have met. Perhaps it is our fate to do so. It seems that the water from Hot Wells is particularly beneficial to a weakness in the lungs, and it is pumped directly to the Clifton houses – for a trifling yearly fee – and I have not even to bestir myself so far as to attend the Pump Room. A strong inducement for me to occupy my family home."

Cassandra compressed her lips. The boyish suitor who had quailed beneath her angry glances had developed into a man impervious to her rebuffs. Her foot tapped now in anger. "I thought you might have sold your Clifton residence, now that you have inherited so many others."

"Certainly not! Some of my most precious moments can be recalled in that house."

Cassandra drew a deep breath. "Will you please go away," she begged. "I . . . I must present an appearance of . . . of decorum and . . . and self-restraint if I am to achieve my purpose with my niece."

"Which purpose is . . .?"

"The same as that of any other chaperone, sir, as well you know. To introduce her to the world, and, I hope, to a man who will make her a good and honourable husband."

"I was unaware that you had a niece old enough to make her Come-out. You see, Cassandra, I have kept abreast of society matters in an exemplary manner."

Her flush was now one of deep chagrin. She could not refute the idea that Susan was too young to bring out. Silently she deplored her niece's behaviour as she said, "I am holding myself responsible for the daughter of my late brother, whose widow is an invalid."

Verax gave her a small nod. "My sympathies went out to your family, my dear, when I heard of his death. As you will recall, Roger was a good friend of mine. Your sister-in-law must treasure his memory."

Cassandra felt a glow of friendship towards him, and for an instant she was transported back in time to the days when they had shared happy hours and childhood sorrows. She turned to face him, seeking the right words, but his next remark threw her again into confusion.

"I know Roger's daughter to be scarcely past sixteen. What reason can you have for removing her so early from the schoolroom?"

"That is no concern of yours!"

He raised an eyebrow. "You may be right. On the other hand, your family and mine were as close as relatives once. I feel a natural care for Roger's only child."

Cassandra struggled to fight back the threatening tears. She knew an intense need for someone strong to talk to. There was no member of her immediate family who was not too deeply enmeshed in problems and duty for her to pour out her doubts and fears for Susan. Loyalty forced her to state mendaciously, "My niece is so mature – so endowed with grace – I decided – we decided . . ."

"Cassandra – if there is any way I can help . . ."

Verax's face was filled with sympathy. She hesitated. He had spoken the truth when he said that their families had been intimates. She searched for words to explain her predicament, yet remain uncritical of Susan. The dilemma was solved for her in the last way she would have wished.

She had not noticed that the music had stopped. Susan's voice broke in upon them. "Dear Aunt Cassandra," she cried in tones so affected that Cassandra almost flinched, "pray allow me to present Mr. Oliver Buckley. Mr. Buckley, my aunt, Miss Cassandra Wells."

In the brief silence which followed Susan's irruption into the conversation, Cassandra was aware of Mr. Pennington's pink embarrassment as he stood a little way behind Susan, and the cool displeasure of Verax. She nodded to Mr. Buckley. "How do you do? I must assume you have made the acquaintance of my niece during the dancing. I do not recall you as being the partner to whom she was introduced by our Master of Ceremonies."

The young man was unabashed. "No, indeed, Miss Susan and I took to one another from the start as we went down the dance. I always know when I am going to rub along with someone, you know."

Cassandra gave him a look which encompassed his expensive, embroidered purple waistcoat, his high collar and voluminous cravat, and the excessive number of fobs and rings which adorned his person.

"I feel sure, sir, that you must have other commitments at the ball, since we have only just met."

"Oh, nothing that I care to keep, ma'am, now that I have met the lovely Miss Susan."

He threw Susan a rapturous look which was received by that damsel in some trepidation, as she was struck by the sudden realisation of her reprehensible conduct. Cassandra was on the point of rising and ordering Susan to accompany her back to their rooms when Verax said, "I feel sure, Mr. – Buckley – is it, that if you consult your memory you will discover an appointment which cannot be broken."

Mr. Buckley's face began to light with his bland smile when he caught the eyes of the Marquis and reddened. "Well, I – that is to say . . ."

"Exactly," agreed Verax. "Pray do not allow us to detain you longer."

Mr. Buckley executed a bow which threatened to hook his dangling fobs and watches to the toes of his elegant dancing pumps and walked away. His place was taken speedily by Mr. Pennington, who assured them that he deplored the incident and that never had he felt so aghast, begging the ladies' pardon until Cassandra graciously said that she felt sure it would not happen again.

"I hope not, Miss Wells, but these days it is so difficult to keep the occasions exclusive when every merchant and farmer's son seems to have the wherewithal to buy his way into society."

He left Cassandra struggling with an array of emotions which threatened hysteria. She had been detected in a lie, since it was obvious that maturity was the last quality displayed by Susan. She had been pushed into discourtesy toward a young man, who, however vulgar, had been led, by Susan, to expect a different reception. And to cap it all, the whole episode had been shared by Verax in whose eyes she wished to retain the dignity of her new status as chaperone.

What a poor guardian he must think her if an upstart like Buckley could force himself upon her so easily! If he had not held her in conversation. . . . In a way it was his fault. She turned to glare at him, and found his dark eyes fixed upon her in an expression of deprecating amusement which told her that he had followed her thoughts correctly.

Before she said a word he threw up his hand. "I capitulate, Cassandra. I took your attention."

He looked at Susan, who was gazing at him in awe. "How are you, Miss Susan? I daresay you do not recall me. I was used to visit your home when you were a child."

"Oh, did you know Papa? I missed him dreadfully, you know – I still do. He always had time to help me with my lessons – I am a hopeless dunce – and he taught me to ride and – oh – everything."

If Verax had been planning any reproach, however delicate, he was coaxed out of it by Susan's artless enthusiasm and sincere expression. Her small face was glowing with health and exercise, and lighted from within by her memories.

The musicians struck up for a cotillion and Verax said, "My medical advisers may rot! There are three couples over there waiting for a fourth! Miss Susan, will you do me the honour?"

And Cassandra was left to contemplate the man whom rumour once had it would rather die in battle than live without her, as he proved that, when not fighting, he had learned to dance with lithe expertise, following the steps of a particularly favoured dance of hers, while Susan dimpled and simpered beneath his smiles in what Cassandra labelled a most affected way.

Lord Verax returned her charge, and although his forehead was damp and his pallor increased, it was easy to believe his assertion that he had not enjoyed anything so well for an age.

He pleaded fatigue and retired shortly afterwards and Cassandra watched him go, wondering why she felt suddenly so weary when almost all she had done was to sit upon a bench and maintain desultory conversation with other ladies.

CHAPTER
THREE

SUSAN'S chatter seemed endless as she scarcely drew breath to regret that the ball ended at twelve o'clock, then continued repeatedly to extol Lord Verax, his person, his wit, his interesting pallor, his valour as a soldier, with what Cassandra decided was an immoderate lack of reserve.

When she pointed out that his lordship was the first worldly man Susan had met, and that when she made her Come-out in London he would not appear so wonderful, her niece refused to believe her. And when Cassandra warned her that she should curb such raptures as gentlemen lost trust in girls without apparent modesty, Susan asked ingenuously, "Do you think Lord Verax believes me immodest?"

"He is old enough to make allowances," replied Cassandra.

"But not too old for me to . . ." Susan stopped, biting her lip.

Cassandra was calm, though her heart had given a jump. "Not too old for you to contemplate as a suitor? You will forget him soon, I am sure."

Lord Verax's conduct could not be said to help dampen down Susan's infatuation. When the two ladies went walking on Clifton Down he appeared, riding his horse with care over the ice-hard grass. He dismounted to join them as they gazed at the obelisk which commemorated the men who had fallen in India and she expressed her commiserations as he looked at the inscribed name of his father.

In memories of their shared past Cassandra could forget for a moment the present increasing confusion of her senses. She looked at Verax's beautiful mare and stroked her nose. "Meet Tiffany," murmured his lordship. "When I was wounded my servant found me because she stood over me."

"So you saved your master's life," breathed Cassandra. "Clever as well as lovely."

"Why, Cassandra, I believe you are really glad I came back," said Verax. Mockery once more sharpened his voice, and she felt a flash of anger.

"I am delighted by the safe return of any gallant soldier, sir."

His eyes held faint triumph at his success in breaching her reserve, and she turned from him in sudden confusion to look again at the names on the obelisk. Images came crowding in; she was recalling the sound of galloping hooves as she and Jonathan tore over the Downs. She felt again the grip of his protective hand as they peered over the sheer side of the Clifton Gorge. She thought with shame of his hurt and humiliation beneath the sneers of sir Vincent Pierce.

"Remembering, Cassandra?"

She saw that he had forgotten nothing. Had he held his anger hot after his public set-down? His mouth curved in an unfathomable smile. He *was* mocking her. She would strike the expression from his face.

"Remembering what, sir? A few childhood

games? It is not easy to recall the past when life is so filled with pleasures."

An artless interruption by Susan ended the duel of words, and Lord Verax almost ignored Cassandra while he indulged in gentle flirtation with her niece.

Watching Susan fluttering her long lashes over laughing hazel eyes, seeing with new perception her niece's petite, dainty figure in soft brown furs the colour of her curls, made Cassandra, tall, more generously proportioned, her hair unfashionably gold beneath the hood of her black ankle-length sables, feel too big and too old.

She realised that until now she had been playing the role of chaperone, and when Verax remounted and left them she walked back to the Clifton Hotel, her innate honesty compelling her to admit that while she had protested her belief in the happiness of her uncourted state, secretly she had expected former beaux to greet her masquerade with derisive laughs and continued admiration – and an attempt at flirtation.

Verax's behaviour had shown her that fickle man was only too ready to take a woman at her word and turn at once to younger, fresher females.

Susan was unusually quiet, and Cassandra glanced down at her. Her perfect lips were slightly parted in a tender smile and her eyes were filled with dreams. Dreams of Verax?

Cassandra was filled with inexplicable fury. So, the little minx was attracted by Lord Verax! Cassandra thought of the man they had just left and tried to picture him married to a witless bird-of-paradise like Susan. It would serve him right if she made London difficult for him by throwing the two of

them together at every opportunity. She might even
drop the odd hint to one or two of the well-known
tittle-tattlers that Verax was dangling after Susan,
then watch his efforts as he tried to extricate himself.
For naturally he would never wish to marry such a
pretty addle-pate, and she must discover as soon as
possible at what part of the Season he expected to
come to town. He must return if only to visit his
physicians.

Life in the following months was going to be very
amusing, she decided, and wondered why she felt so
little real amusement at her excellent plan to tease
and embarrass Lord Jonathan Verax, one-time Captain Ashford, avowed love of Miss Cassandra Wells.

Cassandra decided to take their main meals in the
downstairs rooms, feeling that Susan would grow
accustomed to eating in public places where her
habit of peering curiously at everyone who passed
would be eradicated before they went out in London.

She whispered an injunction to her niece not to
look so openly at a woman whose over-ample figure
was too well revealed by her incongruous Grecian
robe.

Susan smiled. "Oh, Aunt Cassandra, pray forgive
me. I find it all so . . . so . . . captivating."

Cassandra was curious. "Did you learn nothing
from your governess or at your various schools? I was
under the impression that young ladies were
instructed in the ways of society."

Susan looked vague. "To speak truth, I did not
much listen to my teachers. I disliked school, you
know."

Cassandra opened her mouth, then closed it, and
stared at her pretty niece before she said, "Well, I

must impress upon you that if you annoy any of the leaders of female London, you had as well remain in the schoolroom until you are married off to some man of small status."

"Is that so? Well, I will be good." She ended her promise with a little gasp. "Look, Aunt Cassandra. There is Lord Verax. He has taken a table near the window. He has seen us, I think. No! Yes, he has! He is approaching us."

Cassandra remained staring into her wine until she heard Jonathan's voice. "I wondered if you would be here! How charming you both look."

Cassandra glanced up. "We meet again, my lord."

Verax laughed, his dark eyes holding her blue ones for a moment. "It was clearly destined that it should be so." He looked around at a hovering attendant, and Cassandra thought, if he asks if he may join us, I shall refuse him.

Of course, she should have known better than to think that he would commit such a social blunder, and as he bowed and returned to his table she immediately wished that she had desired him to be seated, for now she was condemned to eat her soup and fruit with the knowledge that Lord Verax was behind her, and able to watch her unobserved, except by Susan. That damsel clearly caught his eye whenever possible, and as they reached the end of the meal, raised her glass of ratafia in an answering toast.

As they left the dining-room, Cassandra favoured his lordship with a small bow as they passed his table and he rose to his feet and returned the courtesy, after which she was forced to listen to Susan's raptures as she described to her own satisfaction his lordship's handsome person, his elegant apparel and his courteous demeanour.

The two ladies retired to their respective bed-chambers, where they rested for a while to recover from the effects of their late night and early walk. Susan fell asleep at once, but Cassandra was restless. She made the decision to cut short their stay in Clifton. If there was to be snow the roads might become impassable and she and Susan must get to the leading *modistes* and bootmakers before the start of the season.

She would say nothing to Verax. It would be a relief to be away from his disturbing presence.

And once in London it was evident that Susan would be besieged by young, admiring beaux, which would probably irritate him. It might make him enter the lists to challenge the others for Susan's favours.

It would all be excessively entertaining to watch, decided Cassandra. She and Susan would leave tomorrow.

It proved impossible to leave the following day. Nurse and the maids declared that they needed more time to pack, and while this would not have weighed unduly with Cassandra, Eliza returned from a journey in the hotel gig, after an inordinate length of time, to report that the first and second post-house keepers she had tried had refused to entrust horses and carriages to roads and weather which they insisted were death-traps.

"I persuaded another man to hire us two carriages and the necessary pairs," explained Eliza, "but I had to pay him more than the one-and-sixpence a mile for each equipage and agree to set out at first light tomorrow."

Cassandra fumed at the delay, and was irritable when Susan came out of her daydreams to express her surprise that her aunt needed to hire coaches and horses at all.

"That remark simply proves how unfitted you are to assume care for yourself," retorted Cassandra. "Since I took up permanent residence in Ridgefield I have not needed anything but a gig and one carriage pony and my riding mount. Only those who travel a great deal and who have an abundance of money can keep large stables. As it is, two carriages scarce suffice. Nurse and the maids will have a sad crush."

Susan giggled. "It is lucky that Eliza and Bella are thin."

Cassandra opened her mouth to give yet another lecture on Susan's inability to be serious, then closed it. Perhaps she had best leave her ingenuous niece to develop in her own way, since it seemed that her empty-headed frivolity attracted gentlemen.

The thought caused her to say in carefully casual tones, "By the way, Susan, there will be no need for you to mention our departure should we see Lord Verax today."

Susan's eyes opened wide. "Not tell him! but is not that discourteous? And why should he not know?"

"Our movements cannot be considered of interest to someone who . . . who is here only for his health and . . . and has simply been an unexpected acquaintance," dissembled Cassandra.

"But he *likes* me! I know he does!" cried Susan, going straight to the point which concerned herself.

"Precisely," countered Cassandra. "And if we go
– leaving our regards for the manager to convey – it
may make him all the more anxious to renew your
acquaintance in London."

She refused to listen to the inner voice which tried
to tell her that Verax would certainly enforce the
suggestion that to set forth on a journey in such
threatening weather, when that journey was not
strictly essential, was foolish in the extreme.

Daybreak the following day found her shivering
outside the hotel, staring in disgust at the two "yellow bounders" supplied by the post-house.

"Are these the best vehicles to be had?" she
demanded of the two post-boys, dressed alike in
short boots, tall beaver hats and shabby yellow jack-
ets.

The younger of the two "boys" who clearly would
not see fifty again, touched his whip to his hat. "I
couldn't say that they be the best the master's got,
ma'am, but they be the best he do want to send out at
present. It ain't going to be possible to travel fast, so
't'won't matter much, he says, that the carriages be a
bit past their prime, likewise the horses, he says."

Her attention drawn to the two pairs of animals
harnessed to the post-chaises brought a further
exclamation of disgust from Cassandra and when the
luggage was loaded, the hotel account settled and the
two equipages moved off, she knew with a despon-
dent heart that she had been pushed by her own
feelings into an unwise move.

Her apprehension was justified by the first part of
their journey to Bath, which was conducted at an
agonisingly slow pace necessitated by the icy, deep-
rutted roads. The change of horses and riders took

far longer than usual, and from there they were
slowed considerably as the roads became more difficult and the turnpike keepers more reluctant to
leave their fires. Marlborough was behind them at
three o'clock when she had thought to be at least at
Reading, and the grumbles from the three servants
in the second carriage had reached proportions
which made it difficult to remain polite. She demanded of her latest postillion that he bestir himself,
which, being young and heedless, he did with abandoned enthusiasm so that the second carriage was left
behind in the inn-yard, giving Cassandra a grim
satisfaction at the thought of Nurse's comments.

Her elation did not long survive. The early winter
darkness began to grow with a suddenness increased
by the encroaching trees. The postillion was clinging
gamely to the nearside horse and the carriage
swayed.

"W . . . where are we?" enquired Susan, fearfully.

"Savernake Forest," Cassandra said, "and we
shall soon be in Hungerford, where we will bespeak
beds for the night. That is, of course, if this creaking
vehicle does not give up before then."

Her words, which had been intended to wring a
smile from her nervous charge, proved disastrously
prophetic. The postillion gave a shout of alarm, the
carriage rocked, slid sideways and stopped with a
crunch of breaking wood, as it leaned to a point at
which it must surely have toppled over but for the
sturdy beech tree which held it. Susan began to sob
loudly, and Cassandra stifled a desire to box her ears
as she pulled herself up to thrust her head through
the window.

The postillion had soothed the frightened horses

and twisted his rein in a tree-bough before he came to
enquire after the ladies. Upon behind reassured that
they were frightened but uninjured, he touched his
hat. "Then with your permission, ma'am, I'd best
unharness the horses and go for help. We're nearest
to Marlborough, so I'll ride there."

Susan cried from the depths of the carriage, "You
cannot leave us alone! We are two defenceless ladies!
What of the . . . the miscreants who may come upon
us?"

"I daresay they be all tucked up in their own
houses, ma'am. They'll not be looking for travellers
on such a night. Now don't you fret, missy, I'll get
someone to help you and you'll soon be no worse for
your adventure."

Cassandra by no means shared the post-boy's cer-
tainty that they would be free from molestation, but
she simply said calmly, "On your way back to the inn
you will see a second chaise. Be so good as to inform
the occupants that Miss Wells and Miss Susan Wells
are stranded, but safe. Our maids will be able to wait
with us while you bring assistance."

As the sound of hooves died in the frosty night,
Susan said shakily, "F . . . forgive me, please, Aunt,
for my display of emotion. I had quite forgotten that
the others will soon be here. We shall not be long
alone."

They made themselves as comfortable as possible
in the tilted carriage, pulling their fur lap-robes
about them and huddling together for protection
against the dropping temperature of the air which
came through the damaged window. The only
sounds were of the crackling of the tree branches as
the frost bit deep and Cassandra said with forced

cheerfulness, "As the post-boy said, Susan, this is quite an adventure. You will be able to laugh at it with your friends."

"I . . . I hope so! Indeed, I do, ma'am!"

"Have no doubt of it! What thought you of your first essay into Clifton society? It will be far gayer in town, I assure you."

"I liked it a great deal! Why do you think we did not see Lord Verax yesterday?"

The question took Cassandra by surprise, though it had been annoyingly in her mind until the accident. "I do not know," she said, then added, "Why should you suppose he would visit us? He has acquaintances in Bristol. No doubt he was amusing himself somewhere."

"Perhaps he was unwell. It is not long since he was so dreadfully ill."

Again Susan had touched upon Cassandra's thoughts, and in a vexed manner she said, "I am sure he was not! Verax is an important man now he has succeeded, you know. We are very small in his way of life."

Susan's face clouded over. "I had thought he liked me."

"To be sure he did. Truly, child, you must not be set down by one gentleman's not paying you his whole attention! Wait until you arrive in London! Verax will scarce be able to reach you through your throng of admirers."

"I would always make way for him," muttered Susan, but before Cassandra could give a tart reply to this unmaidenly resolve there was a sound which brought them both to frightened silence. That of footsteps approaching over the brittle grass, and the murmur of men's voices which came clearly through the air. Susan clutched at Cassandra.

"Footpads!" she said in a horse whisper. "Oh, dear ma'am, we shall be robbed and our throats slit. I have heard of such things."

Cassandra removed the grasping hands and stuck her head through the window, to find herself face to face with three men of gaunt aspect and threadbare, soiled clothing. She fought to keep her voice from revealing her terror.

"C . . . can you assist us?" she asked. "As you see, we have met with a mishap. Our post-boy will soon return with men, and our servants are due at any moment, but we are uncomfortably situated at present."

One of the men bent to peer under the coach. "Won't be no use trying to move that, lady. The perch is gone. I daresay it'll have to wait till a thaw before it can be got out, if then. Be your post-boy coming back with another coach for you?"

"Of course he is," said Cassandra, knowing that the inexperienced boy had not even looked beneath the carriage.

"If you knowed the coach was broken why d'you ask us to help you pull it upright then?" demanded one of the others.

The first man, who wore a battered tricorne hat said, "You didn't know, did you? And I'll take a bet your boy didn't know neither. Perhaps he won't come back at all. And I don't suppose you've got servants, else why would you be here alone?"

If Cassandra had had any idea of concealing Susan's presence it was ruined by the girl herself as her voice came muffled by her fur robe, "Oh, please, good sirs, leave us be. I . . . I have not much money on me, but you may have it all if only . . ."

Her voice ended in a quavering shriek as Cassandra reached inside the fur and pinched the first portion of flesh she encountered. "My niece is frightened, gentlemen, as you have gathered. . . ."

"Gentlemen, are we?" demanded Tricorne Hat. "That's funny, that is! We was gentlemen when we beat Boney in Spain. We was gentlemen when England wanted soldiers to fight for her! But now we be no good because disease and wounds have left us too weak to fight, and so we're vagabonds, unfit for work. And our wives and babies be hungry, so we'll take what you've got, and if you hand it over nice and smooth we'll give no harm to you, 'cos we be still men of honour though no longer gentlemen, and . . ."

His words were lost in a gasp which was echoed by Cassandra as a figure stepped out of the trees and a gauntletted hand lifted a wicked-looking pistol which caught the gleam of the last light.

CHAPTER
FOUR

TRICORNE HAT put out his hands in supplication. "Don't shoot, yer honour. We wouldn't have harmed the ladies. Honest to God, we wouldn't!"

"Step back from the carriage," said a voice which made Cassandra start."

"It's Lord Verax," whispered Susan, and Cassandra pressed the girl's shoulder to silence her.

"You men claim to have been soldiers!" snapped the Marquis.

"That's right, yer honour," said the second man. "Soldiers we was, and . . ."

"Pray have the goodness to answer only the questions I ask," Verax said coldly, jerking the pistol and causing the men to cower.

"You say you were injured in Spain! In what battle?"

Tricorne Hat answered quickly. "In the battle for Pampeluna, sir. Byng's brigade we was with. We saw two horses shot under gallant Ross, sir."

"Aye," said the second man, "they say they was using rocks to throw at the enemy before we came 'cos they'd run out of ammunition. Twelve thousand of us beat twenty-five thousand. They said we made old Soult retreat. But the war was over for us three on account of our wounds, and now we can't get work.

Weather's too bad, they say. They never said aught about the weather in Spain."

"Show me your wounds," ordered Verax.

Cassandra's eyes were riveted on the astonishing scene as the first man walked towards Verax, revealing for the first time a disfiguring limp. He rolled up his ragged trouser-leg and the blood-red setting sun flashed between bare branched trees from a rapidly clouding sky, to illumine a wound which had removed most of the calf muscle of his leg, and left deep crimson scars.

Cassandra gulped and turned away, but Verax said, "This wound is still raw in parts. It should have healed if you sustained it as long ago as Pampeluna."

"It's got ulcers on it, sir. I think it's on account of not getting much to eat. It don't get a chance to heal."

Cassandra ventured to look back as Verax gestured to the other men. The second said, "I got mine in the shoulder, sir. One of my arms is still useless."

Tricorne Hat jerked a thumb towards the third man. "He can't speak. His throat was nearly cut through by a bayonet. And he's got some disease that makes him keep shivering. He'll never be no good for soldiering again."

Verax stared at the three men, and Cassandra wondered if a trick of the light had given his eyes a moist look. "Pampeluna," he murmured, as if the name held some kind of magic. "There was a battle! The men who fought that day deserve better from their country."

He reached into a pocket of his heavy coat and

pulled out a purse which he threw to the men.
"There is enough to keep you and your families
over the winter. Perhaps the fates will be kinder
to you when the warm weather arrives. Good food
should help the wound to heal. May God go with
you."

The first man took the purse, and for an instant
the three of them stared at Verax as if he had lost
his reason. Then they appeared to Cassandra to
stand straighter, and the rough clothing became
infused with dignity. As one man they saluted
and turned and marched down the road towards
Marlborough.

Verax put away his pistol and strolled to the carriage. "I gather that you have come to no serious
harm, ladies."

Susan scrambled up to peer over Cassandra's
shoulder. "Oh, Lord Verax, how came you to be
here? How wonderful of you to save us! You are like
one of the knights in shining armour in my old story
books!"

"Do not be absurd, Susan," commanded Cassandra. "You have heard that those men had no
intention of attacking us . . ."

"You are very sure of yourself, madam," said
Verax coolly. "I am by no means so certain of their
good intentions."

"You mean to tell me that you believe they might
have . . . have hurt us in some way, yet you gave them
money and allowed them to go!" Cassandra's voice
rose in her indignation. "What sort of justice is that,
pray?"

"The kind of justice three men who have suffered
and lost so much in the service of Britain richly

deserve. Perhaps they would not have done you mischief – who can tell? They were desperate. You heard them. They have wives and children who starve. They probably have no fuel in their homes, and it is cruelly cold."

Cassandra was more than ever angry. "You could not possibly be certain that those men had been soldiers. They could have received their injuries as footpads."

"They knew more of the fighting than any footpad could have gleaned, and I know a bayonet wound when I see one. And I know also the lengths to which hunger and cold can drive men. I have known both, though not in such dreadful measure as those wretches. While you, madam, know nothing of such matters, and had best allow me to be the judge."

Before Cassandra could argue he said calmly, "I must hope that your footwear enables you to walk for a short distance. Voices carry a long way in this clear air, and my war experiences have made me cautious. I left my carriage about a quarter of a mile away and came on foot. I daresay you would prefer to accompany me than be left alone again."

Interrupting Susan's gasp of acquiescence, Cassandra said, "There is no need for you to concern yourself further on our behalf, Verax. Our second chaise will be here at any time and our post-boy will soon return with help. I thank you for your assistance."

"Pray, do not be so hasty," begged Susan.

"Wise advice," said Verax, "more especially as I know that at this moment Eliza and Bella are tending Nurse, who has a badly sprained ankle, safe in my assurance that I will attend to your needs. They were devastated when I came upon them. Nurse was in great pain, and your maids were trying to find a bed for her in order that they might follow you to apprise you of what had occurred. I undertook the task and, just as I was about to leave, your post-boy who, to do him justice, was genuinely concerned for you, galloped into the yard. Unfortunately his story of the wrecked carriage made the landlord extremely reluctant to risk another coach so late in the evening, and I elected to bring my own to fetch you. I regret there will be no room for your portmanteaux."

Cassandra pushed open the door of the carriage and it swung upwards and outwards. She longed to ignore the hand which the Marquis held out to her, but she knew that the height of the step from the ground was greater than she could manipulate alone. As it was she was in such haste to dispense with his help that she misjudged the jump and landed in an undignified scramble, while Susan, with maidenly reserve and grateful thanks, managed to make the descent with grace.

Verax climbed the step of the tilting carriage and reached in and drew out the fur wraps. "I must insist that you bring these, ladies. My curricle does not afford much protection from the elements."

Susan allowed him to drape a lap-robe about her shoulders as she gazed up at him admiringly. "Have you truly driven from Clifton in an open coach?" she breathed.

"Not quite open. It has a hood," he answered, smiling down at her.

"How strong you must be, in spite of your wound," said Susan

Verax laughed. "I have slept outside in weather worse than this, Miss Susan. A soldier needs strength."

Cassandra took the other lap-robe and ostentatiously carried it over her arm, though a few yards of walking along the treacherously icy road in the freezing air made her wish she had not been so proud. She was making vain efforts to hide her shivering when the first snowflakes fell, and she was glad to climb into the curricle where she and Susan sat close enough to allow Verax to tool his two magnificient greys with consummate skill. She was longing to ask him how he came to be on the road at all, but bit back the words. Not for anything would she allow him to sense her curiosity. Again Susan had no such inhibitions.

In answer to her question Verax said, "I was engaged all day yesterday in business with my lawyer. Imagine my amazement when I arrived at the hotel this morning to find that the ladies had gone! I was bored with Clifton, so I decided that I might as well follow you to town."

"Your valet must have an extraordinary facility for packing to enable you to be so close behind us," said Cassandra.

"I did not wait for him. He is following with my gear."

From Susan's small sigh of satisfaction it was clear she had assumed that Verax had been in pursuit of herself. The idea jolted Cassandra unpleasantly, but she did not say more as the air abruptly became dense with swirling snowflakes which blotted out everything.

Verax pulled the horses to a walk, allowing them

to step with dainty hooves, feeling their way by instinct. "There is a farmhouse a few yards on," he said, "we must shelter there. It would be madness to try to proceed in this storm."

The baying of dogs led them to the farmhouse gate through which Verax drove. He looked at the ladies. "We have a slight problem. Someone must hold the horses' heads while we seek shelter. I think I had better do the asking – we do not know what manner of people reside here. Cassandra, you were always good with horses."

She might have known, she thought, that he would not ask the fragile Susan to perform the part of a groom, but she knew he talked sense and she held the animals steady, murmuring quietly to them, as Verax knocked on the farmhouse door.

There was a pause and a jumble of words she could not catch, before the Marquis returned, followed by a surly farmer and a youth who stared open-mouthed at the elegant carriage and beautiful animals. Verax helped Susan down.

"If you will go inside, ladies, the farmer's wife will attend you. I must see that my greys are suitably cared for."

Cassandra's nerves were stretched, or she would never have said, "You put your animals before us, sir!"

She knew she deserved the glance of surprise thrown by Verax, who did not vouchsafe a reply. Of course he could not leave these high-bred creatures to the attentions of a boy and a man who had probably never handled anything but cows and work-horses! Of course Verax was entitled to expect her to cope admirably with a mere farmer's wife!

She and Susan entered the large, warm kitchen, with its mingled scents of smoking hams and bacon, boiled cabbage, and an unacceptable waft of what proved to be a wet and rather grubby dog. The farmer's wife dropped them a clumsy curtsey which threatened to topple her round frame. "You be welcome, ladies," she said. "What a terrible night it is, to be sure. And what a terrible winter we be having. Will you sit by the fire and drink something? I can offer you mulled ale, or . . ."

"Tea would be most acceptable, please," begged Cassandra.

The woman's eyes widened. "Bless you, ma'am, we don't drink tea. Nor yet your coffee. We be only farming folk. I got some raspberry wine if you'd prefer it."

Cassandra sipped the sweet brew, feeling that she would barter her soul for tea, but the wine was good and gave her a warm glow, and she smiled gratefully at the woman who hovered anxiously near, and at a girl of about twelve who blushed.

"Can we get you some victuals, ladies? We got a very good cheese, and I baked bread this morning. The butter's nice too, and I could cut a bit of ham and fetch a crock of pickled beets."

Cassandra exclaimed, "How kind you are to take us in and to offer us such excellent fare! Pray, what are we to call you?"

"Becky Jones, ma'am, and my man's called Jack and my son's George – after His Royal Highness, the Prince Regent, ma'am, and this is Joan, named after her gran'mother."

Cassandra smiled at Joan, and Susan greeted her with a murmur. Both girls seemed overcome; Joan by embarrassment and Susan by her unimaginably simple surroundings.

Cassandra's lips quivered as she wondered what that portly, though always elegant and witty gentleman, the Prince Regent, would say, could he hear himself compared, however slightly, with the youth who followed his father and Lord Verax into the kitchen.

The farmer's surliness had vanished. "His lordship will take some ale, woman," he commanded his wife.

"Lordship, is it?" She hurried to obey as the three males sat and talked at length about the Marquis's perfect horses. Jack was glowing with delight at housing such creatures, and George stared openly at Verax. Their man's talk continued throughout the unpretentious but delicious meal served by Becky, who sent Joan upstairs after murmured instructions about bedcovers. She then proceeded to wash dishes in a tub of water she had heated over the fire in a black pot, replacing what she took out with cold water fetched by George from the well.

Verax leaned lazily back in his chair. He had removed his long topcoat to reveal buckskin breeches, a black superfine coat, a white cravat knotted in the Coachman style, and leather boots, whose shine, damaged by the snow, would probably cause his valet to weep. He looked perfectly at ease in the rough farm kitchen, and Cassandra remembered that this was a man who had survived many military campaigns. His air of complete *rapport* as he filled a rough clay pipe with tobacco proffered by Jack, and assisted the farmer to fill the kitchen with the fumes of acrid smoke while talking knowledgeably of animals and their various disabilities, seemed only to widen the gulf which now lay between them.

She coughed, delicately at first, then more noisily and Verax glanced at her, a gleam of mischief in his eyes.

"I trust you are not taking cold, Cassandra."

"I think not, sir," she replied coldly, eyeing his pipe meaningly. She longed to make a sharp comment on the manners of a gentleman who would smoke in the presence of ladies, but her duty as guest to the farmer and his wife precluded any such indulgence. Verax could not be considered wrong to fit himself so completely into the humble but welcoming atmosphere.

"I am glad to hear it," Verax said amiably. "I daresay you are weary. You have had a long day, have you not?"

Becky rose at once and Cassandra found herself saying, "I should be most grateful if you would show my niece and myself to our beds. It is perfectly true that we have been on the road since dawn and are tired."

She quelled with a glance Susan's half-expressed desire to remain, and they followed Becky, who handed each of them a candle stuck into an iron candleholder.

The farmer's wife threw open the door of a small bedchamber and Joan looked up from a truckle bed she had just made up. "The young lady won't mind sharing this with my Joan, will she, ma'am? We have few rooms here. Joan will give her bed to Miss and fetch hot water for her, and Miss is welcome to one of Joan's nightgowns which will fit Miss, being so dainty as she is."

"But . . ."

Her protest did not reach him. He made the leap and when she ran to the window he was vanishing into the swirling snow.

CHAPTER
FIVE

INSTANTLY Cassandra was filled with regret. If she could have recalled him she would. She stared, shivering, at the dim outline of the bank a few feet away. It was too far for her to jump and in any case, Becky had taken her cloak and boots to dry by the kitchen range. She would need to go through the kitchen, and she picked up her gown, hesitated, and replaced it on a chair. She shrank as much as Verax from humiliating the kind farmer and his wife.

She resigned herself to bed, consoling herself with the knowledge that Jonathan was a soldier and used to rough shelter, but the memory of his wound and severe illness tormented her, and she lay in the hard box bed, her tired body unable to relax, her brain a jumble of thoughts, until she felt she hated the solid mattress, the scratchy nightgown, the winter storm, Susan who had started her on this ill-managed journey, and, above all, she hated Verax for not persuading her to allow him to stay.

The following morning found her heavy-eyed and hard put to conceal her irritability. She entered the warm kitchen to be greeted by a smiling Becky. "Good morning, ma'am. I hope you slept well."

"Thank you, Becky. It was exceedingly generous of you to give up your own bed to . . . to us. I did not realise . . ."

"Well, we could hardly have a fine lady like yourself and his lordship sleeping on our kitchen floor, now could we, and then, o' course there's our George in the wallbed over there. His lordship's been up since dawn, seemingly, to inspect his horses. He must have crept out like a mouse. The men do love their four-legged creatures, don't they, ma'am?"

Cassandra smiled wanly and seated herself at the kitchen table, where she ate sparingly of new-baked bread, butter and strawberry preserve.

Becky watched her in concern. "Aren't you feeling quite the thing? I'd say you had a good appetite generally."

"I . . . I am determined to cut down on my intake of food. I must be a little more slender for the London Season."

Becky's eyes widened. "Is that so? Well, it seems a shame that a fine figure of a lady like yourself can't eat what she pleases." She patted her own swelling buttocks and grinned. "I never stint meself. My Jack likes me round, he says." Then colour flooded her face. "Oh, beg pardon, ma'am, I shouldn't speak so to you."

Cassandra was saved from replying by the entrance of a yawning Susan. "Hello, Aunt Cassandra. Heavens, I am weary. All that travel – and Joan and I spent an age talking. What an interesting life she leads. She can milk cows and harness a horse to a ploughshare and make cheese and butter and bread. How I should love to do those things!"

Cassandra could not bring herself to reply. The idea of her niece performing any strenuous act other than dancing, or of undertaking farm work when she could scarcely tie her own shoelaces, was too obviously incongruous to need words.

Susan continued, "Perhaps I shall have time to learn if we are stranded here for long."

Cassandra almost dropped a glass of water which she sipped in preference to ale. The idea of remaining another night had not occurred to her. How would she go about reversing her decision to refuse to share quarters with Verax?

She need not have worried. He came into the kitchen, followed by Jack, discussing with him the merits of turnips as opposed to carrots mixed with bran as a relaxing emollient for horses, and smiled at Cassandra.

"Enjoying your breakfast, my dear?" he said, before seating himself by the farmer and continuing to talk of horses, their ailments and their cures, while eating steadily through a plate of ham, bacon and boiled eggs and washing it down with ale. He broke off long enough to look at Cassandra and say, "The snow has stopped and we may soon be on our way, so gather up your things," and Cassandra and Susan were saying their goodbyes in less than an hour.

Just before Verax swung himself into the driving-seat he said to the farmer, "You have been so exceedingly kind to us. I wonder if you would honour me by allowing me to contribute to the purchase of that piece of land you were telling me about?"

Jack muttered, "Well, sir, we didn't do it for gain. We was glad to have you. It's been a privilege, sir." He shuffled his feet. "O' course that land would help me give my girl a good dowry. She'd be well wed then."

Becky's face lit up expectantly and she put one

work-worn hand on her daughter's shoulder while Joan's fair skin flamed into blushes. Verax reached into his coat pocket and he and Cassandra remembered at the same moment that he had given his purse to the destitute soldiers. There was a tiny pause before he looked up at Cassandra and held out his hand. "I left our money with you, my dear."

Cassandra looked down into his eyes. Then with a smile she removed her purse from her reticule, Verax extracted several sovereigns, and Jack took them with a clumsy bow and murmured thanks.

The Marquis handed Cassandra her purse, climbed into the curricle, and in another moment they were leaving the farmhouse, Cassandra and Susan waving to Jack and his family and Verax lifting his long whip in a final salute.

The snow had stopped during the night and lay powdery on the icy roads. Verax held the horses until they had taken their measure of the surface, then he allowed them their heads and Cassandra gazed at their satin coats, gleaming beneath the frost-silvered trees.

"That was well done, Cassie," said Verax. "I shall naturally repay the money I borrowed."

"Not all of it. I would prefer to share the cost which was incurred for my niece and myself."

"I should think so!" cried Susan. "If it were not for us you would probably be cosily ensconced in Clifton."

She gave the Marquis a fluttering of long lashes over coquettish eyes. "And if it were not for you we would be – where, I do not know! Perhaps even now someone would be searching for our lifeless bodies."

Verax laughed, and to Cassandra's over-sensitive awareness he sounded complacently pleased.

"How came you to drive so far in a curricle?" she asked. "I would have assumed you to possess your own chaise now."

"You are right, of course, but I purchased this excellent vehicle from a Bristol man rolled-up by gambling debts, and came to the Clifton Hotel hoping to persuade you to drive with me. I followed you never dreaming that you would have got so far, particularly when the hotel manager waxed indignant over the dreadful vehicles and horses you hired."

"That was not from choice, sir."

"I would not dream of suggesting that it was."

"And why *did* you follow us?"

Verax concentrated for several moments on driving as his high-bred animals took exception to a drift of snow, which fell upon them from breeze-tossed branches of overhanging trees, before he said, "I was concerned for the safety of ladies in such weather. I was able to use my own horses stabled along the route which is how I overtook you."

"I recall the days when you journeyed by stage," Cassandra observed inconsequentially.

"Days now passed, happily for me. I regret the early demise of my relative, but I had scarce ever met him and it would be hypocritical of me to suggest I do not relish the inheritance of an honourable title and wealth which allows me freedom."

He paused and Cassandra stole a look at his face, whose expression did not reflect his words. He stared down at her. "I have not the freedom to return to finish the fight against Bonaparte. That I am sorry for."

"It is your duty now to administer your estates for the good of your people. You have done your share of fighting."

"Yes, indeed," agreed Susan. "I think it wonderful of you to come so far after your recent awful wound."

"I cannot take all credit," smiled Verax. "My head groom is at the inn – he did much of the work. He is an expert, as is the man who will ride Tiffany to London in easy stages."

Cassandra felt a mixture of emotions. When they had climbed into the curricle propriety had demanded that she place Susan on the outside of a seat meant only for two and she was hard put to decide which she found most irritating; Susan's repeated expressions of adulation so serenely accepted by Verax, or the way in which his arm, or knee, or shoulder unavoidably brushed hers as he manoeuvred the horses over the difficult terrain. Each time they touched her heart pounded in an annoyance which his words brought to the surface.

"Grooms? Valet?" she snapped. "I thought you said you had only one servant with you in Clifton."

"One *indoor* man, my dear. My valet. He does not cook, you know. He would think it demeaning, but he is an *artiste* in his care of my clothes."

"Do not tell me you have become a popinjay!"

"I would not for the world make such a claim, Cassandra, but I feel I have a duty to be indulgent to poor Bowler, for my body-servant who has been with me since I took up soldiering is well able to lash him with insults with no help from me. Daniel thinks that a uniform or plain coat is good enough for any occasion. At least . . ." the Marquis paused reflectively, "he was used to think so. Lately I have noticed a tendency in him to listen furtively to Bowler's advice on the knotting of a cravat and the shining of boots. I gather there is talk of a milkmaid he met in Hyde Park. It is truly amazing how love will change a man. He begged me to leave him in London; it would appear there is a prosperous draper on the scene, and Daniel's wooing is at a critical stage."

They had travelled the short distance to the Marlborough Arms where Cassandra and Susan were able to assure their worried maids that they had not spent the night in the carriage, as suggested by Eliza; arrived at the next inn and lain awake worrying over their domestics, as put forward by Bella; or been murdered and their bodies buried beneath the snow, as suggested by Nurse.

The landlord was veering between elation at having a Marquis beneath his roof and the confusion attendant upon hosting an injured and difficult-to-please old lady, while knowing that one of his postchaises was wrecked in Savernake Forest.

Cassandra was intrigued to hear Verax dispose of the landlord, pointing out that if he had hired out a decent, modern, well-sprung carriage steered by an experienced boy and not a heap of ancient wood and a boy still wet behind the ears, the accident would probably not have occurred. And furthermore, he might think himself lucky that the ladies had not been hurt – or worse – in which case he could be facing a lawsuit. And finally, he had no doubt that if he would immediately despatch someone to bring back the ladies' portmanteaux they would feel sufficiently grateful to offer a reasonable reward.

When Cassandra complimented Verax on his

handling of the situation he said shortly, "I have been used to command."

His tone made her look sharply at him and she saw that he was white about tight lips. "You are ill, Jonathan."

"Not ill – only very weary. I shall take some rest now if you will excuse me, ladies."

"Oh, Lord Verax," said Susan, "It is all our fault that you are indisposed."

He gave her a wan smile. "Not so, Miss Susan. When I realised that you had gone so far I could have turned back, but once having begun my journey to London, I decided I might as well proceed."

"And how very fortunate for us that you did," breathed Susan.

Cassandra felt an irrational disappointment at Verax's reply, but it was clear from Susan's expression that she did not believe so casual a reason.

It was necessary to stay at the inn for two days before a local apothecary pronounced Nurse's ankle strong enough for further travel. The Marquis decided that he too would take a rest, and his suggestion that they proceed to London in one party was received by everyone else with such relief that Cassandra submitted. She explained carefully to Verax that it was her duty to follow the wishes of so many women who felt it necessary to rely upon the escort of a man.

"I am thankful that I consider myself equal to any normal problem encountered en route," she said.

Verax bowed. "Then let us join forces, my dear Cassandra, and in the acquired strength and wisdom of our advancing years, we shall shepherd your enchanting little charge and the small army of ancient ladies to safety."

In spite of herself Cassandra laughed. She and Verax were talking in front of the fire of the best private parlour after the others had retired. She was seated in an easy chair and he was leaning on the mantelshelf. He said softly, "You are still the most beautiful woman I have ever met, Cassandra. What a pity to waste yourself in a loveless existence!"

She glared at him, her humour destroyed. "It is typical of a man to equate love with an alliance with a member of the opposite sex. I have love in abundance from my family."

"How quickly you take offence! You used to be quite romantic. Why, I recall that you wept copiously over the sins and sorrows of Olivia when we discovered the *Vicar of Wakefield* and . . ."

"Do not be absurd, Verax! We were children then and behaved as children. Now we are full grown . . ."

". . . and must behave with coldness to one another? Would you have it so, Cassandra?"

A warmth which alarmed her had crept into his voice. She sprang to her feet. "I would be friends with you, Jonathan, so long as you understand that there can be only friendship between us."

"Have I suggested otherwise?"

She gasped. She should not have assumed that his words had held more meaning than they expressed, and she felt suddenly vulnerable – exposed. She said coolly, "Once you quite mistook my feelings for you. I would not have it happen again. I think you could not have enjoyed the experience."

Immediately she wished her words unuttered, bringing with them as they did memories of that horrible scene from their past. She knew that Verax was looking into her face, but she could not meet his eyes.

He said slowly, "Can you be so utterly lacking in the more womanly emotions? I do not want to believe it. Susan could teach her chaperone something, I think."

Furiously she rose and walked to the door, flinging words over her shoulder. "When I need tuition from that chit I will certainly inform you!"

Thanks to Lord Verax, Cassandra and her entourage were supplied with comfortable chaises and reliable horses and the journey to London was accomplished in under two days over roads, iron-hard with frost, which showed further evidence of the severe weather in wrecked carriages and broken portmanteaux and bandboxes. Verax escorted them to the doors of the elegant Park Street house bequeathed to Susan by her mother's parents, and left for his mansion in Berkeley Square, promising to visit them soon.

The butler and housekeeper met them with many exclamations over their protracted journey, and assurances that their bedchambers had been ready for days, and Cassandra was able to take her thankful ease in a charming room furnished in rosewood, deep pink floral hangings and soft carpets of the same pale blue stucco of the ceiling and frieze. She sat in an upholstered gilt chair and toasted her toes by an excellent fire set in an iron basket in the inlaid marble fireplace, while Eliza hung up her gowns. Nurse had been conducted with due ceremony to her own bedchamber with its attendant maid, and had expressed her satisfaction at the very proper arrangements.

The next few days were fully taken up in the essential business of replenishing their wardrobes. Visits were made to warehouses selling muslins, silks and the newly-favoured bombazine; to fancy fringe and trimming manufactories, and to woollen-drapers, for the weather showed no sign of breaking.

Susan was ecstatic. "Just think," she told Nurse, "we have been to a warehouse given over entirely to lace. I tell you, I did not know where to turn."

Cassandra had begun the rounds of *modistes* with the firm intention of rigging herself out in a chaperone's discreet clothes, but she found it impossible to resist her feminine instincts when she entered the establishment at 22, Upper King Street, of Mrs. Bell the famous Fashion Inventress, to be greeted by the cry of, "*Miss Wells!* My prayer is answered. You are the *only* lady who can set this off to its full advantage."

"This" proved to be a hooded, scarlet velvet gipsy mantle lined and trimmed with swansdown. "And for alternative wear I have made a little velvet gipsy hat to match, which you will see is lined with white satin and has matching swansdown trimming."

Having once lowered her guard Cassandra was persuaded with little difficulty to buy a sage-green carriage costume with a tiny cape, and a cerulean blue dinner dress adorned with floss-silk in the shape of shells, and topped by a cap of the same colour ornamented with pearls and a curling ostrich feather.

Even *he* will not be able to make a mockery of that, she thought, immediately banishing the idea as unworthy of notice.

From then on Cassandra chose all her purchases

with an eye to beauty, and none whatsoever to cost or
staid austerity.

The ladies visited Hookham's Library in Bond
Street and chose books which Susan declared she for
one would have no time to read; and Cassandra
purchased tickets for various entertainments.

Once in Bond Street it became imperative that
they should enter Atkinson's famous perfumery and
follow this with a call on Mr. Asprey, where Susan
purchased an Indian coral necklace and several bead
bracelets. "For," as she ingenuously explained to the
startled purveyor, "one cannot be for ever wearing
one's diamonds, emeralds, et cetera!"

In an astonishingly short time gowns were brought
by the dressmakers for final fittings, boots and shoes
delivered, and several dozen pairs of gloves arrived.
The Season would not normally be in full spate until
later, but London was beginning to fill with members of the *ton* who were unable to hunt because of
the weather.

Susan had begged to visit Astley's Amphitheatre,
and recalling her own youthful delight Cassandra
consented and was in the drawing-room awaiting her
charge when Lord Verax was announced.

She was too late to suppress her feeling of elation
that she was dressed in the new scarlet mantle and
hat, and his eyes opened wider, before he swept her a
graceful bow. "Cassandra, I compliment you upon
your appearance. It is nothing short of dazzling.
There is one thing only that . . ."

He stopped and she turned away her head to stare
from the window at the passing of a carriage in the
street below, so that she could hide her chagrined
flush.

Verax continued slowly, "I hesitate to point out the fact, but I do not think you will be regarded as a chaperone if the remainder of your purchases resemble that one."

Cassandra replied casually as she peered down to establish why a post-chaise should have drawn up at the door, "How are you to tell that I have only recently bought this outfit? I might have had it for an age. I have small opportunity in Ridgefield to wear . . ."

He laughed, "Don't try your bamming on me, ma'am! I have had little to do for months but observe my fellow creatures, and I know exactly how the new fashions are cut."

She turned, "Have you called for a particular reason, Verax?"

"That is not very friendly! I came to request the pleasure of your company – and that of your delightful niece – upon an expedition."

"We are already engaged, sir. I purchased tickets for Astley's."

"And your escort . . .? I take it that you are suitably equipped with one, Cassandra, for truly, in that cape and hat you may attract the attention of any male with a good eye for beauty."

She glared at him. "Why must you always be so . . . so mocking?"

"I do assure you it is not my intention." He came to stand by her at the window. "Cassie, give up this charade. If you have decided that you are not attracted by the state of marriage, that is all very well. But you are far too pretty to go around London without proper chaperonage. Why will you not admit it?"

She felt anger flaring at the same time as she

wondered why any reference to her attractions should produce this reaction. She was trying to think of a reply which was too scathing to be countered when Verax leaned nearer the window. "You have guests, Cassandra."

She uttered an exclamation. "Oh, how provoking! Susan is so looking forward to her outing." She gave the lady who had just descended from the post-chaise a closer look. "Why, it is Lady Alethea Whittam! How comes she to be in town? She professes to dislike *ton* society and I know she hates travelling."

"The widow of your cousin, Sir Ralph," said Verax, as they watched, then as the knocker sounded and Cassandra turned away, he said, "The servants are unloading luggage – and a second lady has left the carriage. Oh, that will be her maid!"

Before Cassandra could summon up a reply the door was opened by Wardle, the butler, who announced the visitor.

Lady Alethea, a lady of some fifty-six years, was of medium height and moderately stout. She advanced into the room in a plum-coloured pelisse and pressed her cool cheek to Cassandra's.

"How well you look, my dear cousin." She removed her gloves and handed them to Wardle, dismissing him with an imperious gesture.

"Pray, will you not be seated, Cousin Alethea? You are acquainted with the Marquis of Verax, are you not?"

Lady Alethea chose the comfortable chair nearest the fire and held out a hand. "I have known Jonathan since he was in short skirts. How are you? We have followed your career with interest in our little far-away corner of the world."

"How is Surrey?" asked Verax with only the ghost of an amused inflection.

Lady Alethea had no sense of the ridiculous. "Frostbound, as the rest of the country! A journey of little over three hours has taken almost five. There were times when I thought I would not arrive at all."

"As bad as that?" said Verax.

"Yes, indeed, though you will know since you have all recently come up from Bristol." She shuddered. "How anyone could undertake so long a journey in such weather . . ."

Susan had entered as Lady Alethea was speaking and made her curtsy. Lady Alethea embraced her young relative. "How very pretty you look, my dear. Yellow suits you well. But be sure to wear warm cloaks. I will settle myself in while you are away. No, no, I insist that you go on your expedition. I would consider it my duty to accompany you – weary though I am – were not his lordship here to perform the honour."

"Y . . . your duty?" stammered Cassandra.

"Indeed! I have had communications from both your sister Elizabeth and your brother's widow, Susan's mama, telling me of your sojourn in town. I immediately repaired to Clandon Park to discuss with the dear Countess what I should do – do you know the Onslows, Lord Verax? Tommy Onslow is a noted whip, I believe. When they heard of two young ladies alone in town they were adamant that my duty lay in coming at once to act as chaperone."

"*I* am the chaperone here," declared Cassandra.

Lady Alethea seemed not to hear. "'You must go at once, dear Lady Alethea,' said Lord Onslow," she continued. "He immediately offered me the loan of his best post-chaise. He has always been exceedingly fond of me, you know. Why, if he were not already wed – but enough of that. Away you go, my dears, and I shall speak with Nurse. I know she is here. She will enlighten me as to your activities so far."

She paused to waggle an admonitory finger at Cassandra. "You should have sent for me, you know. You must be aware that I put duty before all. And a child of your dear papa's – there was a time when he was thought to cherish hopes in *my* direction. Well, that is all in the past. I shall begin my task of chaperone as soon as I am rested. I did understand from Elizabeth that you, Cassandra, had some notion of undertaking this business yourself. So good – so unselfish – but truly, dear, I do not think that looking as you do, dressed as you are, it would be considered fitting."

"Just what I have been saying," put in Verax solemnly.

"Spoken like a sensible man, sir. I relinquish my charges into your excellent care."

Verax swept her a deep bow and crooked his arms. Susan placed her fingertips upon one and Cassandra hesitated only a moment before taking his other side. She was well aware by his look of suppressed amusement that he knew just how much she longed to lose her temper with her imperturbable cousin and to refuse his escort. She would not give him the satisfaction of enjoying her discomfiture, and when the coachman had walked the Marquis's elegant town carriage to the door, and a footman let down the steps, she entered and allowed him to cover her with a lap-robe of sheepskin, avoiding his humour-filled eyes.

CHAPTER
SIX

MR. ASTLEY'S entertainments were pronounced a huge success by Susan, who took particular pleasure in the transparent fireworks and the slackrope vaulting. She was as uninhibited as a child, clapping her hands and giving exclamations of joy. Several young men in adjoining boxes, as well as those in the pit and gallery, ogled her freely, and Verax appeared amused by her ingenuous delight. Cassandra saw by his alert glances that he had noted the fact that quite a number of men were giving Cassandra herself a good deal of impertinent attention, but she concealed her relief that the Marquis was there to counter the stares of the vulgar and felt cross with herself for such craven feelings.

Her visit to London was not proceeding according to her plan. In fact, it was becoming as unmanageable as her emotions, which were being lacerated in so many ways that she marvelled at her own inconsistency. She knew she was flattered by the gentlemen's obvious admiration, while despising the originators as strongly as when she had fled society. She felt glad to be gowned so well, while regretting her loss of resolve to garb herself as befitting a chaperone.

Her inability to cope with such conflicting ideas made her quite irate, and she bade Susan show decorum in a tone so abrasive that she knew she deserved the astonished glance she received from Verax, and she arrived back in Park Street in an irritable mood.

Lady Alethea was seated in a chair near the fire in the small drawing-room and she greeted them over her tambour-frame with a bland smile. "So there you are! Did you enjoy the entertainment?"

Cassandra was about to point out that such childish amusements had ceased to interest her, but Susan preceded her with a long and appreciative description of everything they had witnessed.

Lady Alethea finally waved her away. "I have been through the invitation cards on the mantelshelf in the saloon, Cassandra. Most gratifying! I can see that a busy time lies ahead for me. I take it that you will be accepting most of them, though naturally we shall not at first be able to spend a whole evening in one place. Except, of course, in Carlton House. I look forward to seeing His Royal Highness again – I have had the honour of meeting him before, you know. And there is the Drawing Room. You will have begun arrangements for Susan's presentation gown."

Cassandra felt almost drowned in the flow of words. She longed to be able to suggest that her cousin's presence was not required, but could not do so, if only on the grounds of hospitality. And she retained an annoying memory of the forward Mr. Buckley and the ogling dandies at Astley's, and had to admit privately that the presence of a matron would help.

Lady Alethea had not stopped talking and her voice began to lull Cassandra like waves upon a gentle shore until she realised what her cousin was saying. ". . . and who knows, Cassandra, before we are finished, we may also find a suitor for you."

Cassandra's fury was so immense that she shook as she bit back a retort. She would give Lord Verax no notion that she took Lady Alethea seriously.

Her cousin continued, "I believe strongly in the blessed state of matrimony, although I was widowed so tragically early." She held a wisp of lace handkerchief to her eyes for a second. "And it was a sorrow to me that I had no child, though now I sometimes think when I look about me that I should be thankful that I was not favoured. Children can be such a worry, do you not think so, Lord Verax?"

"Indeed, I feel sure that they can," the Marquis replied amiably.

Lady Alethea beamed a smile around the room. "And now we must all do what we can to get this pretty child wedded to a suitable husband, must we not?"

Susan flushed and threw Lord Verax a beseeching look beneath her curling lashes. He spared her feelings by saying gently, "I think Miss Susan will require no assistance to attract a fine suitor. Rather will she need our protection from smitten adorers!"

How discerning he was, thought Cassandra. He knew to a degree when to use his wit and when to be tender. What a lover he would make! The thought escaped her vigilance and it was apparent that it had occurred to Susan, who was regarding his lordship with a dewy-eyed expression of admiration.

The Marquis rose and bowed. "I also have engagements for which I must prepare. I hope that we shall meet somewhere tonight."

The ladies dined alone, and at nine o'clock were

joining the procession of carriages to the door of
Chesterfield House where they spent half an hour
before driving on to the pillared porch of Devonshire
House. Here they were able to alight under cover.
Fog, which had been plaguing London for days, was
growing thicker, and they were glad to take their
places inside in the long line of ladies and gentlemen
who were mounting the famous circular staircase of
marble and alabaster. By the time they had been
greeted by the handsome sixth Duke and the Dow-
ager Duchess, and Susan had been introduced to
several dozen people, they had been over an hour in
the gilded, domed reception chambers and Lady
Alethea declared that they must move on.

Cassandra at once gathered the skirts of her
mazarine blue silk gown and prepared to descend the
staircase, but Susan said plaintively, "I had not
thought it would be like this at all."

"Are you not enjoying yourself, Susan?" asked
Lady Alethea, turning her head so sharply that the
bird-of-paradise feathers in her orange satin turban
fluttered in an instant's grotesque life.

"It is not exactly that, ma'm. It is all overy exciting, but are we never to stay in one place? How can
one ever meet . . . meet friends?"

Lady Alethea drew back her chin. "How is one to
avoid meeting them if one is for ever moving from
house to house?"

Cassandra said kindly, "You will become accustomed to it, Susan, and it is not always this way. Just
now Society is returning to London and it is considered the thing to see and be seen. Quite soon we
shall find ourselves at *soirées* and dinners and the
like, and will spend less time moving on."

"Had you any particular friend in mind?" queried Lady Alethea. "I do not see how you can when you are so newly out of the schoolroom. I take it you were not referring to males!"

"No, ma'am!" Susan's face was pink with blushes, and she looked very young in her simple gown of white muslin as she followed her chaperone down the stairway and received her wrap from the footman who called for their carriage.

There was the usual long wait outside the Sefton residence, and once more they joined a throng which moved slowly up the stairway to be greeted by the Earl and Countess.

Lady Sefton exclaimed with delight, "Miss Wells, how good it is to see you back in Society. You have been sadly missed, has she not?"

She turned to a lady who stood near by and Cassandra made a second curtsy. "Lady Jersey."

"Miss Wells. I had heard you were in town, but someone gave me the odd notion that you were chaperoning your niece, and now I see it is not at all the case. How do you do, Lady Alethea? You are too seldom in London."

Lady Alethea gave a complacent nod. "Lady Jersey; Lady Sefton; may I present my young cousin, Miss Susan Wells? Come forward, Susan, and make your curtsies."

Susan's nervousness showed as she recognised the two ladies as Patronesses of Almack's.

"She is overly young to be out," remarked Lady Jersey. Her stringent tone made Cassandra wince. If the Countess used her sharp tongue in condemnation the vital vouchers would not come their way.

"But prettily behaved," countered Lady Sefton.
"And too personable to languish in the schoolroom."

The Countess of Jersey smothered a yawn behind
her black satin fan. "Heavens, I feel weary already
after keeping country hours." She turned abruptly
to Susan. "How is your poor mama?"

"She . . . she is a sad invalid, ma'am."

Lady Jersey nodded twice. "She was my friend,
and so was your late papa." She murmured behind
her fan to Lady Sefton who smiled at Lady Alethea.
"You will receive vouchers for Almack's, ma'am.
Have we made the right decision?" she continued,
turning to a man who had been half hidden by the
group surrounding the receiving party. Lord Verax
stepped closer to the Countess and bowed.

"Most certainly. How could I say otherwise of
ladies so closely associated with my own family?"

"Ah, yes," said Lady Jersey, "I remember that
you and Miss Cassandra Wells both resided in Clifton in the west country." All sleepiness had vanished
from her at the approach of the Marquis, and for an
instant Cassandra felt disconcertingly bleak as Lady
Jersey smiled at him in a way which left little doubt
that she would favour him as a particular friend.

She followed her cousin from the reception area
and was brought back from her abstraction by a
sharp reprimand. "You are frowning, Cassandra! I
daresay you are tired. I am myself. But I am not one
to allow feelings to supersede duty. And ours is to
partake of society's pursuits, and to display a vivacity
and interest at all times – certainly in public."

Cassandra was assailed momentarily by a longing
to use one of Nurse's pithy comments relating to
wordy folk. She resented her cousin's assumption of

authority over her, and it did not help to know that she was right. She summoned a smile to conceal her incomprehensible gloom, and the three ladies passed on into the large reception room.

It was likely that it was decorated in excellent style, but it was impossible to discern anything through the crush of guests. No one was prepared to risk a rebuff to Lady Sefton. Lady Alethea regarded the company with dignified aplomb. "We shall spend more time here," she announced. "I see many acquaintances."

She was greeted by friends, and Cassandra too was soon being welcomed by contemporaries who were loud in their protestations that London had not seemed the same without her. Susan was kept busy curtsying and smiling and receiving the congratulations of other young females just out of the schoolroom. She soon became the centre of a group of girls and young blades and Cassandra, after running an experienced eye over her niece's companions, allowed herself to be claimed by particular friends of her own.

She found that she was enjoying this essay into public life in an unexpected way when a bosom-bow from former years looked troubled as the people around them parted to allow Lady Sefton to cross the room. The Honourable Mrs. Lydia Strand lifted a large Chinese fan to cover her lips and murmured to Cassandra, "Take heed for your niece, my dear."

Cassandra turned sharply in Susan's direction and saw that the youthful party had been joined by a man whom she had no difficulty in recognising as Sir Vincent Pierce. He looked older than his years and his garb was still more colourful than fashion demanded. Cassandra had time to take in his green velvet coat over a peacock-blue waistcoat, and to notice that he wore his hair curled à la Titus, before the gap in the crowd closed.

"They say he is quite rolled-up, and must marry an heiress quickly or the duns will surely gaol him," said Lydia.

"But I thought I saw the flash of gems – emeralds and diamonds," protested Cassandra.

"All paste, they say, made to delude his creditors. He is dreadfully wicked – I would not care to have him paying attention to any female relative of *mine*. Have you ever noticed, Cassandra, how often young ladies find the most sinister of rakes attractive?"

Cassandra did not need reminding that Susan was easy prey for a man with a glib tongue. She tried to see Lady Alethea who, once primed to the danger and armed against rebuff by her invincible belief in her own correctness, would find no difficulty in ridding Susan of anyone considered unsuitable. But her cousin was hidden, and Cassandra heard Susan's laugh trilling above the chatter. Heads were turning in her direction, and reluctantly Cassandra began to make a way through to her niece.

The other young people had moved away, either voluntarily or following intervention by their guardians, leaving Susan alone with Sir Vincent. It was impossible not to stand close to one's neighbour, but there was in Sir Vincent's proximity to Susan an air of intimacy which he had conjured out of years of experience in the beguiling of women. Susan was gazing with a kind of fearful attraction into the lined countenance of a man whose seniority and air of worldliness she clearly found intriguing.

Cassandra said with assumed gaiety, "Why, Susan, there you are! Good evening, Sir Vincent. How kind of you to give your time to my little niece. Susan, you must not monopolise Sir Vincent, whose many old friends surely require his wit to enliven the evening."

She laid a tiny fraction of emphasis on the word "old". It passed Susan by, but Sir Vincent received her speech with a twisted smile on his thin lips and a glitter in his eyes. Now Cassandra was close, she could see that the colour in his cheeks was created by maquillage and that beneath the makeup he was livid, and she found no difficulty in believing Lydia's assertions about his desperate state. She felt a stab of real fear for her niece as Sir Vincent threw Susan a conspiratorial smile which was returned with sympathy and admiration.

Cassandra was at a loss. Sir Vincent was as impervious to strong hints as Lady Alethea, though in his case his obtuseness was deliberate and malicious. Susan saw only that she had attracted a man of fashion whose appearance and smile gave her a deliciously new thrill.

Sir Vincent rendered Cassandra a small bow. "How charmingly you have weathered the years, Miss Wells. It seems only yesterday that you were making your own Come-out, and now you are shepherding this pretty lamb into the wicked world."

He laughed, and Susan's clear trill rang out again. One or two members of the Dandy Set began to pay them particular attention, scenting as sharply as hounds after a fox that incipient gossip material lay within their grasp.

Then to Cassandra's relief a sympathetic face came into view as Lord Verax sauntered from among the crowd and said smoothly, "Ah, Miss Susan! I have been searching the rooms for you. What a crush! There is no doubt that London's hostess of the night is Lady Sefton, but how hot it is! I am persuaded that you require refreshment."

He appeared to become aware of Sir Vincent's presence for the first time. Slowly he raised his eyeglass and regarded the baronet. "It is *indeed* you, Sir Vincent. I scarce recognised you."

A flush ran under the paint on Sir Vincent's lined skin. Lord Verax had neither said nor done anything untoward, but his manner, his delivery of words, his commanding attitude, were calculated to deliver a subtle rebuff.

"Captain Ashford! I beg your pardon – Lord Verax – you have come into an inheritance, have you not? How fortunate some of us are to acquire nobility and wealth."

"And how much better are some of us at preserving the dignity of name and the protection of riches."

Sir Vincent smiled thinly. "It seems that Wellington's army is producing men of words."

"Lord Wellington's army is producing men!"

Verax's voice was too quiet to be caught by the Dandies who were now unashamedly listening, but Sir Vincent's eyes glittered more brightly. Had the Marquis's glance gone briefly over the bright silks and velvets of his garb, the flashing paste jewels? Verax himself was so plainly dressed in black and white that he might have been considered drab were it not for the obvious fact that his coat and pantaloons had been fashioned by *artistes*. One gold fob adorned his white marcello waistcoat and he wore a gold ring with a black pearl.

He held out his arm to Susan. "Shall we go to partake of lemonade? It is being served in the supper room."

Cassandra watched the byplay with an icy tingling down her back. It seemed as if the past was repeating itself. Not quite, however, for the bashful, awkward youth had become a man well able to defend himself from a barbed tongue and a cruel mind, and Susan was behaving better than her aunt had done. Affected at last by the atmosphere, obviously puzzled, yet she had sense enough to place her fingertips upon the Marquis's black coat-sleeve.

Then Verax looked at Cassandra and she saw the hesitation depicted on his face as he wavered in his resolution. Only a second passed before he turned to escort Susan to the supper room, but it made her devastatingly aware that the Marquis had forgotten nothing of the scene on the balcony on that distant night in Clifton, and was as unequipped now as he had been then to gauge her reactions to him.

Toughened soldier, man of the world, distinguished and clever he was, but she still possessed the power to undermine his confidence. And she turned her mind aside from the wayward idea that his presence gave her a sense of incompleteness not compatible with her view of herself as an independent woman. As she watched the crowd close behind Susan and Verax, Sir Vincent held out his arm. "Shall we follow their example, Miss Wells?"

It was becoming like a nightmare. She sensed rather than saw the watchful eyes of the Dandies, and the quizzing glasses being levelled in her direction. She could not refuse Sir Vincent when to do so would create that tiny friction upon which society gossip was founded, and, with a sense of the inevitable, she placed her gloved hand upon Sir Vincent's arm and was led by him into the supper room, where she was forced into partaking of refreshment with him, knowing that Lord Verax and Susan were a few feet away.

She had not realised how minutely she observed them until Sir Vincent said close to her ear, "They would make an excellent pair, would they not? Two highly desirable fortunes, unexceptionable birth, and he with his knowledge of life to tame such a wayward kitten."

She deliberately turned her back on the other couple and dragged a light laugh from the depths of her social awareness. "Do not be absurd, Sir Vincent. Susan is too young to be considering such an attachment."

Sir Vincent raised a white hand on which the false jewels gleamed, and turned his wine-glass slowly so that the claret caught the light of the many candles. He appeared to be engrossed in assessing its quality as he said, "Rumour has it that Miss Cassandra Wells has brought her niece to town most reluctantly, in an effort to wed her before she makes a disastrous match for herself."

"Rumour is so often wrong, Sir Vincent," retorted Cassandra, and managed again to laugh before she sipped her wine. Neither of them seemed to have a taste for the array of pastries, creams and cold meats set out on the long table, although Susan was eating with all the appetite of a healthy sixteen-year-old and she knew that Lord Verax was amused by her.

Sir Vincent smiled. "There is not a woman in England who would turn aside from the contemplation of an alliance with the Marquis of Verax, ma'am. Several of the chaperones here have turned colour with envy and exasperation at his obvious *penchant* for your niece."

She knew he was trying to provoke her, and she made her next laugh so clear and amused that it *must* have reached Verax's ears. "Society is all a game — somewhat like chess. Tonight Verax chooses to amuse himself with my niece, and the chaperones are annoyed. Tomorrow he may pick some other beauty, and I daresay I shall feel equally chagrined."

"Tonight Lord Verax chose to cut me out with a deliberation of insult that will have escaped no one, Miss Wells. I shall not forget."

His words were accompanied by a laugh as bright as the one she had given, and Verax must surely imagine that she and Sir Vincent had much in common.

Lady Alethea pronounced it time to depart soon after supper, and never had Cassandra been so thankful to leave a party. The evening had been a disaster for her! Driving home in their carriage, Lady Alethea stated her entire satisfaction at their first essay into society. Susan was full of praise for the delights enjoyed and those to come. Only Cassandra remained silent, and through the wakeful hours of the night she lived over again the past humiliation she had inflicted upon young Jonathan Ashford and the aftermath of misunderstanding which had crystallised tonight.

But the dissatisfaction seemed all on her side. Verax appeared perfectly content in Susan's company. It was not for Miss Cassandra Wells to question how it was that many men seemed to find their happiness with young ladies who had beauty of body without perspicacity of mind.

She could not analyse her own confusion. She knew only that she wanted to hide from it. She could, she supposed, leave Susan in the care of Lady Alethea and return to her quiet home in Ridgefield, but the idea was cancelled immediately by the knowledge that her cousin's complacency was too long established to be disturbed. Susan might amuse herself with half the seducers in London and that lady would gaze upon her with unperceptive eyes. Cassandra could not abandon her beloved brother's child to such a chaperone.

The only escape lay in marrying Susan off as quickly as possible and, at present, she knew only one man to whom she felt able to entrust Roger's daughter. Lord Verax filled the role of eligible husband to perfection. In spite of her assertion to Sir Vincent Pierce, she knew that the Marquis's seniority was no barrier. It could, in fact, be an advantage in the case of such a gadfly as her niece. She must encourage him to court Susan with all the subtle persuasion at her command, and then she would be free to live her life in the way which most appealed to her.

CHAPTER
SEVEN

THE decision brought Cassandra an uneasy peace, and she managed to drowse her way through the night to be awakened by Susan who entered her room with Eliza who carried the tea, and plumped herself on the edge of her bed.

"Wake up, Aunt Cassandra! Have you forgotten the Fair?"

Cassandra pressed her fingers to her forehead above eyes which felt gritty with weariness. She pulled herself up and lay back on the lace-trimmed pillows. "Fair? What can you mean? There are no Fairs in London at this time of the year."

"The Frost Fair! Oh, surely you cannot have forgotten."

Cassandra recalled that Lady Alethea had mentioned something on their return home last night, as Susan chattered on. "Lord Verax is going to be there and – oh, all London! The Thames has quite frozen over and travelling folk have been arriving by the dozen with all manner of amusements. Several people have said that the ice must surely melt soon. We *must* go today."

Cassandra smiled wanly. "Very well. Dress warmly! I will rise as soon as I have drunk my tea."

Susan disappeared to put herself into Bella's capable hands, and as Eliza began to lay out a soft cream wool gown Nurse bustled in, carrying a pair of blue-and-white striped stockings. "It's a good thing I finished these for you, my lamb. I never heard the like! Walking about on a frozen river! It'll be a mercy if you aren't all drowned."

"People do not drown on ice," murmured Cassandra. "To please you, Nurse, dear, I will wear a pair of your stockings."

Nurse looked both gratified and disappointed and Cassandra said with more warmth, "They will be ideal. Thank you for the good thought."

Nurse beamed. "And Bella is making certain that Miss Susan has a pair also." She hesitated before she said, "You don't look the thing this morning. You're not taking a chill, are you? Because if you are . . ."

"I am perfectly well – only a trifle tired."

Nurse snorted. "All this town gallivanting! I thought you said you was past the age. Why can't we go home and leave that silly chit of a niece to Lady Alethea? It's not as if you was dangling for a husband – and quite right too!"

She glared in the direction of Eliza, who was placing the stockings over the gown with a look of distaste. The maid said with asperity, "I fail to comprehend how you can make such a judgement since you have never been wed, *Mrs*. Webster."

The emphasis on the courtesy title was calculated to throw Nurse into a spasm of fury. Eliza claimed to have been married for a matter of three months to a sailor, who had been drowned and left her to bear a stillborn child. It happened before Cassandra was old enough to remember, and was a matter of extreme irritation to Nurse.

Both women began to size up one another like a

pair of spurred fighting cocks, and Cassandra knew
that it was time for one of her telling interruptions.
She held a hand to her forehead. "I think I may have
the headache coming on," she murmured.

Her handmaidens became instant allies in the face
of this threat, and when Cassandra was in the carriage with Susan she felt the real benefit of Nurse's
soothing potion and Eliza's competent massage as
well as the warmth of her furs and pre-warmed half-
boots.

Lady Alethea had announced her intention to go
to a silk warehouse to purchase material for her
Court gown ."I visited the Frost Fair of 1789, and I
recall I got chilblains – such a plebeian complaint for
a lady – and besides, I have nothing fit to wear for
Susan's presentation."

Susan lifted her skirts now and giggled at the
expanse of woollen stripes exposed. "Have you got
them on too? Isn't Nurse droll! And Bella has made
me don an extra petticoat. I feel as encumbered by
clothes as a lady of ancient days."

They alighted from the chaise and stepped gingerly upon the ice amid a cacophony of shrieks of
children on the swinging boats, the cries of vendors,
the rival music in dancing booths and the braying of
donkeys which were giving rides.

Susan was in ecstasies. She clasped her hands at
the cleverness of a dancing bear, bought a ballad
from one of the printing presses and a pamphlet
commemorating the occasion, and paid a shilling for
a slice of hot roasted sheep. Cassandra's worries
faded as she became infected by her niece's merri-
ment. They met many acquaintances enjoying this
rare spectacle on ice, and Cassandra was not sur-

prised to find Sir Vincent Pierce making his bow to them. He was warmly clad in a redingote with a satin collar, and Cassandra was interested to see that Susan glanced furtively down at her feet to make sure that the unfashionable striped stockings were not on display to the sophisticated baronet.

It would have seemed churlish to resent his joining them casually on so informal an occasion, especially as he accepted gracefully Cassandra's refusal to allow him to take them into a gaming booth. Cassandra was marvelling at Susan's capacity for looking enchantingly pretty while nibbling hot gingerbread and a sugar-plum when Lord Verax, fashionable in a deep caped carrick, black leather boots and a beaver hat, strolled up to them. Cassandra wished momentarily that Sir Vincent Pierce had not been with them, but Lord Verax bowed to the ladies and greeted the baronet with courtesy. The four of them wandered on and Susan's pleasure was so infectious that the awkwardness was almost removed for her aunt.

Once or twice Cassandra thought she felt drops of rain, but concluded that the moisture must be from mist formed by the cold and the fires of the vendors, until Verax suddenly grasped her arm urgently as a report cracked through the air.

"Is someone shooting?" asked Susan.

"Leave the ice immediately!" ordered Verax, and began to hurry them to the shore.

Cassandra thought of the dark, fast-flowing waters of the Thames beneath their feet and felt quite weak, but she maintained her smile as she caught Susan's arm and pulled her along.

They were not too soon. Verax left them on the bank listening to more ominous breaking sounds while, to Cassandra's horror, he stepped back on to ice which was degenerating into a number of moving floes. Both ladies turned frightened looks towards Sir Vincent, who muttered something beneath his breath as he looked resentfully after the Marquis. Then he gave a slight shrug and trod gingerly on to the ice, returning shortly afterwards with two women and several wailing children.

Verax ushered a number of people to safety before all became confusion as the quality rubbed shoulders with the proletariat in a mad scramble to firm ground, and Cassandra held Susan's shaking form close when the girl hid her face in her aunt's shoulder as several people were tumbled into the river.

Verax saw them into their carriage before leaving them to drive himself home. The ladies were pulling away from the scene when they perceived Sir Vincent walking and Susan rapped to halt her coachman and leaned from the window. "Have you brought your own carriage, sir?" she asked.

Sir Vincent smiled deprecatingly. "I no longer keep one, ma'am. But I shall soon find a coach for hire."

"Oh, but you must allow us to help you! Pray, step into our carriage. There is plenty of room."

Sir Vincent's eyes flickered towards Cassandra, who managed to smile. The elegant town equipage did indeed have room for him and it seemed unmannerly to refuse him a ride, though she could not like the idea.

Their journey home was a sad anticlimax to the expedition. Susan said often that she prayed no one had been hurt, and gazed at Sir Vincent with her expressive hazel eyes big with admiration. "You were so courageous to return to danger," she breathed, "and so was Lord Verax. Such admirable behaviour. Confess you were a little nervous! Who would not have been?"

Sir Vincent gave Susan an engaging smile. "I must own I have had a fear of fast-flowing water since I was an infant, but I could not remain inactive while others were in danger."

Susan became even more laudatory about his behaviour and Sir Vincent accepted her admiration equably. When she and her aunt arrived home she told the exciting story to Nurse with exclamatory accounts of the heroism of Sir Vincent and Lord Verax, while Nurse dispensed hot drinks and uttered remarks about folk who tempted the wrath of the Lord by trying to walk on water, which was not natural and never meant to be done by mere mortals.

Lady Alethea declared herself surprised that Cassandra and Susan felt too shocked to attend the evening's entertainment. "I cannot conceive why you should be so upset! You had a fright, I agree, but no one of your acquaintance was drowned. In fact, I have it on good authority that only a few travelling showmen lost their lives."

She went to an Assembly which later she declared to have surpassed all other social occasions so far in the Season, and said that Lord Verax had been present and expressed his disappointment at the absence of the young ladies, while professing to appreciate the delicacy of their sensibilities. She had accepted his invitation to them all to join him on the following night at the Drury Lane Theatre.

Gowned for the Play, Susan looked enchanting in an opera dress of white gauze over white satin, one of the recently invented *chapeau-bras*, in blue, sitting delightfully upon her soft curls, with twilled sarsnet scarf, reticule and dainty kid slippers to match. A single strand of diamonds set in gold encircled her neck.

Cassandra, in her new-found resolve to allow Susan to display her charms to Lord Verax in unrivalled splendour, gowned herself in chestnut brown lace over a cream satin slip. She wore an amber necklace and instructed Eliza to draw her hair back in severe fashion, permitting only a few curls to fall from a simple clasp of brown silk flowers and silver wire.

She was ready first and descended to the small drawing-room to find Verax waiting. He looked distinguished in his plain opera dress of black superfine as he bowed, before looking at her with a smile in his eyes.

"It is of no use, Cassandra. You could wear sackcloth and still your beauty would not be hidden."

She smoothed her cream gloves. "Pray, do not be absurd, Verax!" She found it necessary to concentrate on the removal of a wrinkle in the kid encasing her arm as she sought to mask the pleasure she felt at his compliment. She was relieved that further talk of an intimate nature was prevented by the entrance of Susan, who received her share of appropriate comments on her appearance.

Then Cassandra found she needed all her control to prevent her amusement from gaining expression as the next few moments were enlivened by the Marquis's achievement in agreeing with Lady Alethea that her outfit of plum satin, and high headdress of dancing ostrich plumes, was entirely becoming for an opera box, while managing to avoid being mendacious.

The play was *The Merchant of Venice*, and Susan surprised Cassandra by her close attention. At the end she said, "What an interesting experience. Hugh used often to talk to me of Shakespeare's work, but I never understood before why he loved it so."

"You and Hugh discussed Shakespeare?"

"Why, yes, Aunt Cassandra. When we were younger he told me much of his lessons with his papa. I have always liked Hugh, you know." A pensive expression filled her eyes for a moment before it was banished by the entrance to their box of a young, and most acceptable, Viscount who begged to be allowed to take Miss Susan for refreshment before the start of the Pantomime. Cassandra felt the need only for exercise, and leaving Verax to procure a water-ice for Lady Alethea, she paced along the wide corridors behind the boxes. She was soon joined by the Marquis.

"What thought you of the performance, Cassandra?"

"Poor Mr. Huddart has an awful task in portraying Shylock after Kemble and Cooke, but I thought he made a brave showing."

"Indeed he did. I saw John Kemble play Hamlet when I was a boy, but I have had small opportunity for theatre-going for some years."

There was an awkward silence as Cassandra recalled again the reason for Verax's sudden departure from England. "Did you never meet a lady who attracted you?" she asked suddenly.

"I met many such ladies, but felt no inclination to settle."

"Now you have inherited large estates it is your obligation to marry and produce an heir."

Verax gave her a sidelong look. "May I consider that an offer?"

She looked sharply at him, met the mischief in his eyes, and turned away. "Now you are being absurd again."

"Since we seem to be in a confiding frame of mind, perhaps you will allow me to enquire if any gentleman has ever touched your heart?"

"None! I have never been in love."

"That does not surprise me."

She stopped walking. "Why, sir, what do you mean?"

"What did *you* mean, Cassandra?"

She resumed her walk with quickened steps. "Only that I am not the kind of woman who needs the support of a male."

"That is what I meant," he agreed equably.

"This is foolish talk!" declared Cassandra.

"I did not begin the subject," he reminded her as they turned at the end of the corridor to retrace their steps.

"That is a frivolous answer, sir. A man may consider marriage to quite a late age, whereas a woman should always accept advancing years with a realisation that . . . that . . ."

She glanced at him, wishing she had not entangled herself in a sentence she found difficult to conclude.

Verax was paying her exaggerated attention. "Do go on," he begged in fascinated tones.

She almost stamped her foot. "Jonathan, for heaven's sake! You know perfectly well what I am trying to say and that it is true. A man in your high position has a bounden duty to his family to produce sons. A lady such as myself may choose solitary bliss."

"Ah, but have you considered that if my deceased relative had argued as you do I would not now by Marquis of Verax, and that there is a young hopeful who must be praying daily that I continue in the same 'solitary bliss' so that he will inherit? How unkind of me to disappoint him!"

The corridor was emptying of people. Verax was laughing, and Cassandra had a sudden longing to laugh with him as she had done when they were children.

Verax had been watching her face and he took a step nearer. Cassandra knew a moment's panic at what he might say when all else was driven from her mind as she saw Susan hurrying along attended by Sir Vincent Pierce.

They all met at the box door. The two gentlemen afforded one another the smallest of bows and Cassandra almost pushed Susan into the box, followed by Lord Verax. The performance was about to begin and Cassandra's enjoyment of the amusing Pantomime, *A Trip to Japan*, was quite spoiled in her annoyance at Susan's repeated indiscretions.

There was no chance to question her niece at the supper given by Mrs. Lydia Strand, and it was not until Lord Verax had bidden them goodnight at their front door, and a sleepy footman had taken her elegant cream velvet opera-cloak, that she was able to insist that Susan should accompany her into the small drawing-room.

Lady Alethea followed and stared as Cassandra raged at Susan. "How dared you exchange a partner

I approved for a man like Sir Vincent Pierce? It is not the first time this has happened! You are well aware of the rules of behaviour and etiquette. Soon I shall not risk allowing you out of my sight!"

Susan flushed. "That is unjust, Aunt. Lord Cole went to bring me a glass of lemonade and I did not see him again. A clumsy person stepped on my toes and someone else splashed me with wine. See here – this stain will probably never come off, and this is a favourite gown."

She was close to tears as she displayed the pink patch on her white dress. "Sir Vincent procured me the attentions of a cloakroom maid and escorted me back to the box. That is all."

Lady Alethea drew in her chin. "It seems you are being hasty, Cassandra. Verax spoke of the crush in the refreshment room."

"And besides," continued Susan, with a sniff, "Sir Vincent is not at all as you seem to think. On our way back he was most gentlemanly and kind, especially when I told him about Hugh. . . ."

"Susan! You did not reveal the attempted elopement!"

"Of course I did not! I am not so bird-witted. But he seemed to comprehend how I had cared for Hugh, in a way you never did. He sees me as a woman of feeling. It is no wonder that they call you the Crystal Venus when you do not understand . . ." Her words faded before the fury in her aunt's face.

"They call me *what*?"

"Oh, Aunt Cassandra, I do beg your pardon. I did not mean . . . Sir Vincent said . . ." She paused.

"*What* did Sir Vincent say?"

"Only that in the . . . the clubs – they – the men –

call you the . . . the Crystal Venus. I think it is because you do not fall in love."

"*Infamous!* That he should repeat club gossip . . . that I should be so labelled!"

"They do not mean to be unkind, Aunt Cassandra."

"It seems that you had time to talk quite a lot on your brief walk back to the box. Did he let fall any other gems of knowledge?"

Cassandra knew that she was reacting wrongly. She should allow Susan to follow her obvious inclination to drop the subject, but she could not control her unruly tongue.

"Well, Susan? I await your answer."

Susan moved the toe of her blue pump along the pattern in the carpet. "If you will have it . . . he mentioned something about 'Frozen Wells'."

It was easier to lose her temper over something other than Susan's revelations. "What a shocking lack of decorum! He should have found your proper escort, not brought you back himself."

Lady Alethea said, "It seems a mish-mash about nothing to me, Cassandra. Susan has not done anything so bad, after all. And your nickname is not a dreadful one. When I recall some of the names the gentlemen have thought up for ladies! Why, Venus was a lovely goddess and crystal is very pretty."

But so cold – so glacial, mourned Cassandra inwardly. And *Frozen Wells*! Then she took herself to task. She had not been meant to learn of this, and the names were not insulting. She had made it obvious that she did not wish for lovers, so why should she mind when her rebuffed admirers gave her what they considered apt titles?

She wondered if Verax had heard them, and concluded that he must have. Perhaps he even used them.

"Go to bed, Susan!" she said irritably. "I wish I could impress upon you that your conduct at all times must be circumspect."

Lady Alethea protested. "What has the child done? Sir Vincent is from an unexceptionable family. I know he has been wild, but so have many men who settle when they grow older, or when they marry." She raised an imperious hand. "No, do not interrupt me, Cassandra! I am, after all, many years your senior. Sir Vincent is invited to most of the best houses. We must remain upon terms with him."

"Then I shall bid you goodnight!" exclaimed Cassandra, and retired to her bedchamber, where she tried to see herself from outside as an icy unapproachable woman.

From that time on they seemed to meet Sir Vincent constantly and always, whether at a rout or musical entertainment, a ball or a *soirée*, he came to Susan's side, and since Lady Alethea refused to show disapproval there was nothing Cassandra could do. Her only consolation was that if Lord Verax was present when Sir Vincent tried to monopolise Susan – and he appeared with increasing frequency – he joined them and vied for Susan's attention. His behaviour was a model of discretion, and usually there were other admirers of Susan around, but the keen-eyed Dowagers and the Dandy Set were becoming amusedly aware of the subtle rivalry.

Cassandra stayed in the background. The knowledge of her secret titles, coupled with her disinterest in any man who made even the most tentative of approaches, led to her being taken more and more at her word.

Yet in spite of achieving the kind of success of which every young girl dreamed in her first Season, Susan seemed less vivacious than Cassandra would have expected. She learned to flirt with admirable discretion, playing off one devoted swain against another; managing even to hold Verax and Sir Vincent to her side without obvious friction. But when the ladies were at home her eyes were often sad in a grave face. If she was taxed with being melancholy she laughed at once and declared, with some truth, that she was only tired, being unused to such late hours and so many activities.

The weather continued cold, but Cassandra was accustomed to exercise in the fresh air and had managed to walk part of each day, if only among the shops.

After luncheon one March afternoon a hint of frosty sun tempted her to consider Hyde Park, and she asked Susan to bear her company.

"Oh, Aunt Cassandra, pray excuse me," begged her niece, "but truly I do not feel well – not well at all. I think I would like to go to bed. Bella may bring me one of Nurse's potions."

Cassandra immediately laid aside her grey, furlined mantle and placed her long fingers for a moment on Susan's brow. "You are over-heated, my dear. I agree that you must go to bed, but of course I shall not leave you. I have been concerned for you for some little time past. If you do not show signs of recovery I shall ask Sir William Knighton to call. He is the best physician in London."

Susan gave a wry smile. "Only the best for me, is that it – or are you thinking of poor Mama?"

Cassandra had indeed had her delicate sister-in-law in mind. She did not possess enough medical experience to know if a heart complaint could be hereditary, but she would take no chances with the health of her niece.

Susan took her aunt's hand and pressed a kiss to it. "Dear Aunt Cassandra, you are a better guardian than I deserve. I beg you to take your walk! I am only a little out of sorts, I promise you. It is the excitement, the late hours. Why, I heard of a young lady only yesterday who already has had to return to the country on a repairing lease." She smiled. "I can understand now why you considered me young to withstand the rigours of the Season."

Cassandra longed for her walk. Hyde Park would surely tempt few visitors in such inclement weather, and she felt she might be able to disentangle her thoughts in solitude. Her maid was a woman who kept her own tactful counsel and allowed her mistress the luxury of silence. She looked again at Susan, who seemed to have regained some colour, then she rang for Bella and gave her instructions that Miss Susan should be tucked up with hot bricks at her feet and back, and given warm milk to drink.

Bella hesitated and seemed about to speak before she gave Cassandra a small curtsy and accompanied her mistress from the room.

Cassandra stood for a moment fingering the swansdown edging of her mantle, then she shook off her vague disquiet and sent for Eliza. One or two other hardy souls were strolling in the park, but she recognised no one, and among the great trees she took deep breaths of cold air and pushed her worries to the back of her mind. A solitary mounted figure appeared in the distance and she knew instantly that the rider who guided his horse with such experienced care over the hard earth was Lord Verax.

Suddenly she wanted to call to him, but she knew she must not, and her inability to reveal to him the truth which had become abruptly clear expressed itself in a silent wail which echoed in her head with such insistence that it seemed impossible he should not have heard. Formless words trembled on her lips. Formless because she dared not give them meaning. If she did they would tell them both truths about herself which she did not want to know. Truths too late to know, for Jonathan Verax was going to offer for Susan.

But he must not speak of that today! Not now! He must wait until she was calmer. The Crystal Venus they called her. How they would laugh if they could see into her mind!

He rode nearer and she looked briefly into his eyes, then fixed her gaze on the leafless trees behind him. He must not read what she could not admit to herself.

She felt his gaze upon her face and held her features coldly rigid. He bowed, raised his crop in a salute, and cantered away down the tree-barked avenue.

She swayed and Eliza stepped close. "What is it? You haven't taken Miss Susan's fever, have you?"

"I am perfectly well," said Cassandra, "but it is colder than I had realised. Let us hurry home."

The butler took her cloak and Cassandra walked into the small back morning-room where the remains of a fire still smouldered. She felt she could not face Lady Althea, who was sewing in the small drawing-room, or Nurse, who might come upon her at any time if she went upstairs. She sat staring into the heart of a tiny glowing coal; she paced the room as if she would escape from her thoughts, but no matter what she did, the words which she had been holding at bay were filling her mind with meaning.

I love him, she thought. I love Jonathan Verax! I always have. I humiliated him and sent him away. He obeyed me and that piqued me. Of course I could never countenance another suitor! It has always been Jonathan.

His name filled her brain; his image took possession of her heart. What a fool she had been! She could have held him to her side all those years ago if pride had not prevented her from sending him an apology. And she could have drawn him to her again if she had not been so blind. All her protestations about the blessed state of spinsterhood had been defences for her own stupidity. And soon she would be forced to listen to his declaration of love for Susan and have to watch their joy.

There was a tap on the door, followed by Bella's hurried entrance. Cassandra was about to order her to leave when she caught sight of the maid's frantic face.

"Oh, Miss Wells – oh, what a dreadful thing! I half suspected something – but how could I have known? Why did I not tell you of my worries? I blame myself. Why did she not take me with her?"

Cassandra stared in alarm. "Has something happened to your mistress?"

"Yes, indeed, it has! She told me not to disturb her

again until the morning, saying she would sleep, but I crept into her room to make sure that all was well. I thought there was something odd about the figure in the bed, and discovered it to be only a bolster!"

"A bolster! Where is my niece?"

Bella held out a screw of paper. "I searched about and found this tucked behind the clock in the saloon, almost hidden by today's invitations. It is addressed to you."

Cassandra opened the torn sheet and read, 'Dearest of Aunts, Pray forgive your penitent niece, but I could bear no more. I have gone to the man I love. It is useless to ask for your consent, and I cannot endure life without him. I do so truly care for him, and he for me, and he needs me.'

The paper had been dragged roughly from a writing tablet. Clearly Susan had been in desperate haste.

Cassandra held to the back of a chair. "How much do you know, Bella? What suspicions have you? Miss Susan talks of running away to the man she loves."

Bella twisted her hands. "Lately she has spoken often of someone . . . she said he understood her . . . she talked of him when I brushed her hair." Tears spilled down the maid's cheeks. "Oh, my poor little lady! I have heard such tales of him . . .! But she said he was only a friend."

"For God's sake! Who . . .?" A dreadful thought gripped her. "You cannot mean . . . that rake . . .!"

"Sir Vincent Pierce, ma'am. She kept talking about him and his kindness. And once when I entered her room I thought she was burning a letter, but she remarked only that the fire was low. I didn't want to suspect her. Oh, Miss Wells, if only I had mentioned my doubts to you!"

A chill crept round Cassandra's heart. "You should have done so. You know Miss Susan's propensity for getting into scrapes. Oh, but this is not a girlish escapade. It is dreadful! You could scarcely have foreseen such a disaster!"

"Oh, no, and I did hope that being in London would steady her, especially when I heard that nice Lord Verax liked her. I prayed he would win her. I never could have guessed she would run away with a man like Sir Vincent."

"They must be stopped," said Cassandra.

"But how? She has left no clue to her whereabouts."

"They will make for Gretna Green if they are to be married quickly."

"But what if he is only toying with her? She wouldn't be the first he's ruined, by all accounts."

"Of course he will marry her. She is an heiress."

Bella wrung her hands. "That's true, ma'am, but she's taken the best of her jewels with her. If he sells them he may decide he has enough money to keep him going until he finds someone richer. My dear little lady's fortune isn't near as big as some. What if he abandons her, after . . . after . . . Oh, Miss Wells, I don't know which would be worse for her! A life laid about her in ruins, or marriage with that monster. I've heard accounts of his cruelty."

She finished on a shuddering sob, and her distress forced Cassandra to a measure of calm. She must make a plan of action immediately. Sir Vincent Pierce would enjoy destroying her niece's future, if only to spite Lord Verax. She thought of the foolish,

innocent Susan in the power of a depraved man like
the baronet and resolved that she would discover
where they had gone and follow them. Somehow she
must arrive in time to save her niece's honour. She
could not seek help. There was one man only with
whom she could have entrusted such a secret, and he
was the one in all the world who must never find out.

Susan was making it all too terribly clear that she
did not return Jonathan's love, and if Cassandra was
fortunate enough to save Susan he must not be
allowed to declare himself. But never, if it could be
prevented, would he find out that the girl he loved
had been in the power of the man he most despised.
He must not be hurt and humiliated again.

CHAPTER
EIGHT

FOR a few moments Cassandra considered various courses of action, while Bella went to enquire of Wardle if Sir Vincent Pierce had called that day.

The maid returned to say that the baronet had been shown into the saloon half-an-hour after Miss Cassandra had departed. Lady Alethea had gone to greet him only to find that he had left without paying his compliments. "Very indignant her ladyship was, Miss Wells."

"That is nothing to what she will be if. . . . Return to your duties, Bella, and say nothing to anyone. You must conceal Miss Susan's absence. If she is still in London we may contrive to bring her back quietly. Send Eliza to me."

At the idea propounded by her mistress Eliza was scandalised. "Go to a man's dwelling unchaperoned! You can't do it, Miss Cassandra!"

"I must – there is no one else."

Eliza wrung her hands. "But you don't even know if it's Sir Vincent that has got her. And if it isn't . . ."

Cassandra hesitated, a worried frown on her brow. "Of course, you may be right, but Bella has said that he is the only man who seems to have been engaging her thoughts. Also, if Sir Vincent truly is a friend . . ." She paused. It was difficult to imagine the baronet a real friend of anyone. "I shall have to go to see him. I will decide what to do when I arrive."

Eliza was not so easily persuaded. "At least take a couple of footmen with you!"

Cassandra shook her head. "There is still hope that I may avert a scandal. Eliza, I trust you, but if you will not come – and I cannot go alone – then I must ask Nurse, but . . ."

"Nurse!" Eliza's voice rose to an indignant squeak. "She would make such a bother that the whole household, and then the world, would know. She would not mean to. . . !"

"Exactly! And on whom else can I rely if not you?"

In the face of this telling argument Eliza became acquiescent, and shortly afterwards they were in a hackney carriage being driven to Sir Vincent Pierce's house in Piccadilly.

Eliza rapped sharply on the knocker and the door, which showed signs of neglect in peeling paintwork and unpolished brasses, was opened by a footman in shabby livery. He seemed unsurprised to see two ladies on his master's doorstep, and gave them a perfunctory bow as he showed them in. Cassandra flushed at the implication inherent in the way they were being received.

"Is your master at home?" she enquired.

"Not he! He left not an hour since."

"Will he be returning shortly?"

"Couldn't say, miss. He don't tell me where he's going, but I know there's no dinner ordered, though that ain't nothing new. He always eats in other folks' houses when he can."

Cassandra looked about her at the worn drapes,

the undusted furniture, and remarked the absence of ornaments. Sir Vincent's father had been a noted collector, but she supposed everything to bé pawned or sold.

She thought of Susan in the clutches of so desperate a man and almost groaned aloud. The footman lounged against a door-jamb, pushing a grubby fingernail between his teeth, and Cassandra lost her temper.

"You will remain in an upright position and show me respect while I speak to you!" she snapped, and the footman leapt to attention. The insolent look left his face as he became aware that he was dealing with a lady of quality and not some abandoned doxy.

"B . . . beg pardon, ma'am, I'm sure. I meant no disrespect."

"Is there anyone here with whom your master may have left his direction? It is urgent that I speak with him."

"Well, ma'am, there's the fat old cook, but she's dead drunk, and a couple of women who wash and scrub, and me. Sir Vincent can't keep servants and . . ."

"Pray, do not burden me with your master's shortcomings! Has he taken his travelling carriage out of town?"

The footman shook his head. "If he's gone anywhere it'll be in a hired coach. Come to think on it, he did take a portmanteau."

Cassandra felt near to despair. She could not enquire at all the London posting-houses. She produced a gold coin and the footman's eyes glistened.

"There's his friend in the library. He might know."

On the library sofa lay a snoring man whom Eliza shook awake. He begged for brandy before executing a clumsy bow as Cassandra demanded to know the whereabouts of Sir Vincent.

"Urgent, is it?" he leered. "You don't need him, my pretty. Sir Thomas Aldred – at your service. I'll take good care of you."

Ignoring Eliza's indignant snorts, Cassandra forced herself to continue gently, "Can you direct me to him?"

"Will you remember me later?" grinned Sir Thomas.

"I shall not forget you," Cassandra promised grimly.

Sir Thomas chuckled evilly. "He's making for his Sittingbourne estate in Kent."

"Was . . . was he alone?"

Sir Thomas lurched close. "You'll be looking for a young female? An innocent with brown curls and big trusting hazel eyes? No name, o' course, but would the letter 'S' mean anything?"

Cassandra's lingering hopes were destroyed. Susan had absconded with Sir Vincent.

"Will you be going after him?" Sir Thomas winked. "I'd give a monkey to see his face when you arrive!"

Cassandra could not bring herself to reply and she and Eliza left.

Now Lady Alethea had to be told, and she received the news of Susan's flight and Cassandra's plan to follow her with a mixture of reactions. Disbelief was followed by bewilderment at the shocking behaviour of a man of good family. Then she waxed eloquent on the subject of Susan's lack of thought for her relatives' nerves, and coupled this with the expense of the newly-purchased silk for a Court gown which would not be needed. "For of course Queen Charlotte will not receive a disgraced female and I have no one else to present. If only we could send for a male relative! I should come with you."

She half-rose, then sank back with a low moan, a hand to her eyes. "I cannot! Oh, my poor head! Such a journey in this weather! Such a mission to try to accomplish! My feelings are too delicate. . . ."

Cassandra knew a strong impulse to shake her cousin, and Eliza went upstairs to fling a few necessaries into a portmanteau without letting Nurse catch her. They were gone in half an hour and in three and a half hours were being directed by a villager to Latchet Manor, the baronet's country seat.

Seeing the man spit into the ground after mentioning Sir Vincent's name did nothing for Cassandra's mounting terror that they would arrive too late to secure Susan's honour.

The manor which had been the pride of the Pierce family for generations showed the same signs of neglect as the town house, and as the post-chaise was driven through an archway over cobbles before the main door Cassandra's heart began to pound. The place looked deserted, and she stepped down, followed by Eliza, and paused before instructing her maid to pull the bell ring.

The chimes sounded hollow, and for a moment there was silence. Then the two women heard footsteps, and with a suddeness which was terrifying the double doors were thrown open and the light of many candles streamed across the courtyard. Cas-

sandra blinked, before she asked the footman who
stood revealed whether or not his master was at
home.

"He is, ma'am. Please to come in."

Cassandra told the postillion to walk the horses
and stepped inside the hall, followed closely by her
faithful maid. The door was shut behind them with a
loud bang, and she stared disbelievingly at the scene
before her.

In the Great Hall an oak table was laden with
partially consumed food and bottles of wine, and a
number of men, in various stages of intoxication,
were rising to bow and grin meaningly at her. From
this confusing array stepped one she knew.

"Sir Vincent . . ." she said uncertainly. She could
not think of a way to proceed. It seemed she had
disturbed him while engaged in entertaining his
friends. Yet Sir Thomas had been so exact in his
description of Susan!

"Servant, ma'am," and Sir Vincent swept her a
bow. Cassandra realised that he was sober and knew
by the look on his coldly smiling face that he had
expected her.

Seriously afraid now, she said in low tones, "May I
speak to you privately, sir?"

He responded by waving his hand in the direction
of his friends. "These gentlemen are in my entire
confidence, Miss Wells. You may talk freely."

Cassandra took a step towards him. "Sir, it is a
matter of a lady's honour. I beg for but a moment of
your time."

Her voice could not have reached the men who had
re-seated themselves and were passing round the
bottles of wine, but Sir Vincent said in clear tones,

"The matter of a lady's honour must concern us all, ma'am."

There was a burst of laughter, then a watchful silence, and Cassandra flushed. "Very well, Sir Vincent, it seems I must ask my question in the company of your acquaintances. Have you brought a certain person – a young lady known to us both – to this house today?"

There was a second burst of laughter. Sir Vincent answered smoothly, "One lady only have I enticed here today, madam, and she does not consider herself so young. At her advanced age she sees fit to repel all those who would make themselves her loyal slaves in love."

It did not need the arrival of the gleeful Sir Thomas at that moment to underline to Cassandra that she had been lured here by the devil who stood grinning at her. She felt dizzy with outrage.

"Clever, was it not?" said Sir Vincent. "Welcome to my home, Miss Wells, or may I address you as Cassandra, since we are about to become more closely acquainted?"

Cassandra answered through dry lips. "I cannot imagine what you should mean, sir. My carriage is awaiting me. I shall return at once to London. I came to you seeking help as Miss . . . the young lady's friend." She put a hand to her head. "What can have become of her?"

Eliza brought a chair and Cassandra, in spite of her desire to remain on her feet before the ghastly company, sank into it. The maid stood protectively near her mistress and demanded, "What have you done with our young lady? Have you had a hand in her disappearance, you wicked wretch?"

Sir Vincent's brows were raised. "Do you allow your servant so to address her betters? She needs a lesson." He turned to grin at an elderly painted beau. "She's not young, but she's still comely."

Cassandra felt Eliza go rigid with shock. She rose and stood gripping the chair back. "You make sport of us, Sir Vincent. It seems I have been mistaken. We shall take our leave. I owe you – an apology." She made for the door, motioning Eliza to follow, and heard the sound of her carriage on the driveway.

Sir Vincent's voice was smooth. "Too late, I fear. Your chaise has gone. And now, Cassandra, I will grant you a private interview. Pray accompany me."

Cassandra stared towards the table where a dozen pairs of merciless eyes regarded her. Then she looked at the white-faced Eliza. She had led her maid into this hell's brew. "I will follow you, sir, but I must ask you – implore you – to leave my maid unmolested. She . . . she simply obeyed my orders . . ."

She was disgusted to hear her voice break on a sob and saw that it had not escaped Sir Vincent, whose eyes narrowed in pleasure. "Better and better! How far will you go to rescue those you care for? Truly you have played my hand with me all the way."

He looked at Eliza. "Go with my man to the kitchen. You are safe so long as your mistress pleases me."

Eliza took a step towards Cassandra who waved her back. "Do as he says. I will take care of myself, never fear."

Her words were brave, but she could think of no way to free herself from the situation. The baronet led her upstairs into a drawing-room where a fire burned brightly. "Pray, be seated, Cassandra. I had this chamber especially prepared for you."

"For me? How. . . ?"

Sir Vincent seated himself and lounged back, his fingers toying with the black ribbon of his quizzing glass. "Yes, I will give you an explanation. The realisation of your compliance will add piquancy to my conquest of your charms.

"Miss Susan is taken with some young cub at Oxford – a rector's son. She has bored me with her raptures. I think you might have allowed her to become betrothed to him – and what you could have saved yourself! However. . . !" He shrugged. "I opened Miss Susan's letter and found that the delectable girl had heard that her Hugh was ill, the result of juvenile larking by the river. He fell into the cold water and has a feverish lung disorder."

"I do not believe you! How can she have known any such thing?"

"She wrote clandestinely to him. She is a naughty minx, is she not, but adorable. She has been bribing her footman to bring her any letters from Oxford."

"I cannot think *Hugh* would do anything so underhand."

"You are correct – such a dull fellow he must be! He wrote only once to Susan, protesting his constancy, but refusing to correspond without the approval of her guardians. The letter with news of his illness was penned by a friend. You will have gathered that I tore off the explanatory part of Susan's note. Poor Hugh, it appears, is delirious and crying for his lady-love."

"But we would not have prevented her going in this case!"

"Precisely, my dear, but the young are so impetuous and quite exhaustingly full of movement. Upon reflection I am pleased I shall be allied to you."

"Are you mad? Nothing would induce me to allow you to . . . to place a hand upon me."

Sir Vincent smiled in a way which made her shiver. "Oh, I can assure you I would have no problem in placing a hand upon you, my dear Cassandra, though it is scarcely necessary to do more than hold you here. In that way I shall gain the person of the most beautiful creature in London, and we shall learn together whether ice or hot blood runs through the veins of our Crystal Venus.

"My friends have seen you arrive – they have watched your ascent to the upper chambers with me. Three of the most garrulous have engaged your chaise to take them to London. Your maid is with my servants in the kitchen. Oh, Cassandra, there will be such talk! By the end of tonight all London will be abuzz with the news that the lovely, cool Miss Wells is with me in Sittingbourne."

"My friends will not believe ill of me!"

Sir Vincent continued, ignoring her assertion. "My remaining guests will leave at first light. You will inform them that we are betrothed. If you do not, your reputation will stink so vilely that you will beg me to marry you. I will do so, and you and your desirable inheritance will be mine to command. I would prefer a greater fortune, but a man must seize his chances where they offer, and let the devil take care of tomorrow."

"You serve your unholy master well," said Cassandra, her cool tones belying her terror. "But I could agree to a betrothal now and then deny it."

Sir Vincent grinned. "So you could. And I can just picture the ladies whispering behind their fans, their eyes appraising your beautiful body, while they wonder . . . I can hear the veiled insults of the town beaux. My friends will fan the flames of scandal for ever, and I . . . I will play the part of a lover discarded by his mistress. I do not think you will be able to return to London in your unattached state, do you? I think perhaps the news of your shame may soon reach even your friends in Ridgefield."

Cassandra gripped the arms of her chair until her fingers hurt. "You are wicked – far worse than ever I knew."

Sir Vincent crossed one leg encased in yellow pantaloons over the other and lay back even more at ease. "I have heard it all before."

"How can you behave so? You are of gentle birth – of an honourable family."

The baronet shrugged. "A man grows in the way fate decrees. And so does a woman. I took your measure well, did I not? I guessed you to be a female who would run to help someone she thought needed her, and you were taken in completely. Your friend, Verax, would not have been so quickly deceived. I wondered if you would seek his help, but I had to risk that."

He leaned forward a little. "Why, Cassandra, I vow your countenance changed colour at mention of his name. How much do you care for him? Enough, anyway, to try to hide Susan's flight and return her unsullied to him." He laughed. "It all adds flavour to the enterprise."

A servant brought refreshments and Cassandra shook her head at the food, but accepted a glass of

wine. It warmed her blood, which seemed to have
become ice-cold. She wondered if an appeal to the
baronet would be worth while – perhaps an offer to
pay his outstanding debts – but a glance at his face,
full of malicious enjoyment, stopped her. Why ask
for more humiliation?

"You should eat," Sir Vincent said softly. "Surely
you are hungry. So Junoesque a lady must enjoy a
good appetite."

She remained silent and his laugh sent shudders
through her. "I sense much in you that you try to
hide from less discerning men. You like your food,
your comforts, and it is said that the carnal appetites
are linked. How much I shall relish testing the truth
of that statement."

She was unable to bear more. She leapt to her feet
and made a run for the door in an endeavour to
escape the menacing eyes and lashing tongue of her
tormentor.

Sir Vincent moved faster. He caught her in his
arms and she panicked and began to struggle. She
was tall and strong, but no match for a man who,
despite his dissipations, had sparred with Gentleman
Jackson in his Bond Street pugilistic school, and
rode hard to hounds.

He twisted her arm behind her back and pushed
her to the wall, using their combined weight to prevent her moving, then he captured the hand which
sought to strike him. With his right hand he grasped
her hair and jerked back her head so that he could
stare into her eyes. She saw his enlarged pupils and
sensed his cruel excitement.

"You are terrified, Cassandra! Only of me – or of
all men? Is that the secret of your glacial reserve?

Better and better!" He gave a soft laugh. "So you will pretend a betrothal and play me false, will you?" he grated. "Did you truly think to treat me with such disdain? By tomorrow, madam, you will crawl to me, I promise you!"

He tugged her hair so sharply that she cried out in pain before his lips came so close to hers that she could feel their warmth. As she gave a despairing moan she was released so abruptly that she almost fell. She gasped for breath, rubbing her cramped arm. Sir Vincent's head was raised.

"I thought I heard a carriage." He gave another mocking laugh. "Perhaps more of my acquaintances have come to see the sport." Then came yells and the sound of crashing furniture. "What the devil. . . ! Damn their drunken brawls!"

Someone raced up the stairs. The door was flung open and Cassandra caught a glimpse of a dismayed footman before he was hurled to one side and Lord Verax stepped into the room.

His face was tense with fury as he bowed. "Good evening, Cassandra. I trust you have taken no harm?"

"Jonathan! Thank God you have come! But how. . . ?"

"I am here, which is all that matters. I know you are ready to leave."

Sir Vincent's eyes were narrowed slits of hate. "Miss Wells will not be departing for quite some time, my lord. You are trespassing, and if you do not immediately quit my home I will have you thrown out."

There was a creaking of old floorboards from the landing and a sound of wheezing breathing, then Sir

Vincent's eyes opened in horrified disbelief and he went a sickly yellow. Cassandra whirled to see His Royal Highness, the Prince Regent entering the room. Instinct alone bent her in a curtsy; the Prince gave Sir Vincent a disdainful glance before offering her a plump hand and raising her to her feet.

"Do not be perturbed by my appearing, Miss Wells. Lord Verax was attending me when he received your chaperone's note. He became so agitated that I insisted on knowing what it contained, and overrode all his objections to my coming to your rescue."

He patted the hand he still held. "I deeply regret that a so-called gentleman should have mistreated one of our most beautiful subjects." He released her hand at last and wiped his perspiring brow with a snowy handkerchief. "There is nothing I would not suffer for one of the fair sex."

Cassandra murmured an appropriate response and curtseyed again. Sir Vincent would have appeared to be turned to stone were it not for his moving eyes. The Prince ignored him and continued to smile at Cassandra. She saw that he had gained considerable weight, but "Prince Florizel" had retained his charm. Her mind began to work again and she thought, with relief, that at least the arrival of the Prince would preclude any idea of a duel. This comfort was soon snatched from her.

"Were it not for your presence, sir . . ." said Lord Verax.

"Consider me not here!" commanded His Highness. He seated himself in a corner of the room. "'Pon my soul – little did I think that my boring evening would be so enlivened. A duel! Of course! It is years since I was engaged in anything so romantic."

Cassandra stared at the three men. They seemed to regard it as a game. "Please, sir, no . . ." she begged.

The Prince tutted. "This is a man's affair, ma'am. You must wait downstairs."

He turned to Sir Vincent who said, licking his lips, "We cannot draw swords in your presence, sir."

The Prince said coldly, "Not craven, I trust? You have my permission to fight. I shall stay to see fair play."

During the men's preoccupation with the rules Cassandra stepped back into the shadows. She would not go. Verax was still suffering from the effects of his wound. If he should be bested. . . ! She vowed she would leap in front of his opponent's sword if necessary.

Verax called, "Daniel!" from the doorway, and an immense man appeared. His brown eyes were alert beneath a shock of greying hair. He handed his master a length of rolled leather and withdrew, closing the door.

The Marquis untied the roll to reveal two scabbards from which he unsheated identical smallswords. Candlelight glinted on the wicked-looking tapered blades, and caught the scrolled brass decoration and the copper gilt guards. Sir Vincent managed an amused laugh. "You came prepared for sport."

"You will not be talking of sport when I have done," promised Verax, as he removed his boots.

Sir Vincent responded by taking off his buckled shoes. "Have you considered that I may destroy you? I am an expert with the small-sword."

"Which is why I chose it."

Cassandra's throat went tight. Jonathan would surely be affected by his illness! The Prince was licking his lips, clearly anticipating the fight with pleasure. The duel could be short – and bloody!

CHAPTER
NINE

LORD VERAX and Sir Vincent circled, taking each other's measure, and Sir Vincent ventured several exploratory beats on the Marquis's blade. Verax tore the baronet's shirt-sleeve and he became more guarded; then, seeing an opening, he parried Verax's sword and touched his shoulder. The Marquis's riposte was perfect and Sir Vincent sprang backwards.

The Prince gave a grunt of appreciation and Cassandra glanced at him. His eyes were gleaming. He was lost to everything but enjoyment of the fight.

Every movement was magnified by shadows on walls and ceilings. They fought until both men gasped for breath and perspiration moistened their skin. They were matched in skill, but Verax looked dangerously pale.

Sir Vincent's lips curved in a sneer of triumph. He lunged, there was a lightning movement by Verax and the baronet's sword clattered to the floor. Verax turned his wrist in tierce and the point of his blade was at his adversary's throat. The two were motionless and Cassandra dug her nails so hard into her palms she pierced the skin. Then Jonathan's sword flickered, and a shallow cut was drawn in a crimson streak down the cheek of his opponent.

"Oh, well done, sir," cried the Prince, hauling

himself to his feet. "Exactly what I would expect from a gallant soldier!"

Lord Verax bowed to the Prince and spoke softly to Cassandra. "Bring me his sword." She obeyed shakily, and he wiped both points and replaced the weapons in their scabbards.

"Remember I could have killed you and did not," he said to Sir Vincent.

"I shall forget nothing," rasped the baronet.

The Prince and the Marquis walked downstairs, discussing the duel as if they had just witnessed it in a playhouse. Cassandra felt close to hysterical laughter at the sight of the former revellers at the table rising to their feet and bowing to the Prince, while two burly footmen in Verax's livery stood by the front door and Daniel broke off cleaning his nails with a wicked-looking knife to leap to attention.

"We are leaving," announced the Prince. He gave the diners a frigid glare. A sound from the landing made them look up to see Sir Vincent holding a crimson cloth to his face and staring down with hatred.

Verax held out his arm to Cassandra. "Come, my dear. We must return with all haste to London. Tonight you must appear at some function."

"But your wound," she protested. "You will fall ill again."

The Prince intervened. "He is right, Miss Wells. My presence here will not save your reputation, but by the grace of God Polite Society does not bed itself till dawn."

Outside, by the flare of flambeaux, Cassandra was shocked to see coachmen, footmen and outriders around the Prince's carriage as well as Verax's own carriage and servants. She stepped into the Marquis's coach with Eliza and Verax, and the procession proceeded down the drive.

"I wonder you did not sell tickets," she muttered.

Clouds hid the moonlight and she could not see his face, but his voice held humour. "I could not stop His Highness. He set his heart on saving a damsel in distress. Do you realise this is the third time you have become embroiled in a dangerous situation?"

"A consequence of my venturing into the *ton* world," retorted Cassandra. "Would you have had me ignore Susan's plight? Well, I believed she needed help. . . ."

"Sir Vincent contrived the whole thing cunningly," conceded the Marquis. "By the way, where is Susan?"

"Oh, it is only one of her scrapes," dissembled Cassandra.

". . . I have gone to the man I love . . . I could not endure life without him . . ." quoted Verax. "Come now, Cassie, I am not a fool."

"How did you read her note?"

"Lady Alethea's plea was so incoherent that I went to the house. She showed me the scrap of paper."

"Oh! Well, she has gone to Oxford. Hugh Egerton is ill . . . she is always fancying herself in love . . ." She stopped. Her wits seemed to be deserting her. With every word she was making things sound worse.

She thought Verax's breathing became laboured, and assumed that he was hurt by Susan's behaviour, but when they stopped in Rochester to change horses she was startled to see by the light slanting from the inn that his brow was beaded with perspiration and that he was very pale.

"Jonathan! You are ill!"

"I am all right. We must press on. . . ." His glass of brandy slipped from his hand, and Cassandra caught his head against her shoulder as he slipped into unconsciousness.

Eliza's shrieks for help brought Daniel who lifted his master easily and carried him up to bed. Cassandra had forgotten their illustrious companion until he appeared in the inn, causing the innkeeper to drop a tray of glasses. She sat waiting for a physician by the Marquis's bed while the Prince was conducted to a private room and brought the choicest wines in the cellar.

Verax opened his eyes and smiled weakly. "I regret this display . . . you may leave me with Daniel. Go to London. Your reputation . . ."

He had difficulty in articulating, and Daniel said quietly, "He has done everything he was told not to do. Now it looks as if the fever's returning."

Misery flooded her as Daniel continued, "You should obey him, miss. He always knows best."

"I shall stay!" she said. "He did not fail me and I shall not act in a lesser manner toward him."

A young apothecary arrived and held Verax's wrist in capable fingers, ignoring the Marquis's grumbles as he listened to Daniel.

"I see. My advice is to keep the patient warm and allow him a reasonable amount of fresh air. Often-breathed air has a noxious quality. Allow him to eat, or not, as he chooses, but no wine or spirits."

Verax snapped, "You may address me, sir. I have not lost my ears."

The apothecary bowed. "The attack is by no means desperate, but you need careful nursing."

"I daresay you will fill me with your foul medicaments!"

Cassandra marvelled how the most sensible man could be petulant when ill as the apothecary said mildly, "Drink plenty of barley water – I will send you a Syrup of Endive which will help – if you take it."

When Daniel left to fetch the medicine Verax said to Cassandra, "You will oblige me, madam, by driving with all speed to London."

"And you will oblige me, sir, by remaining quiet. It will be small wonder if your wound has not opened."

"Hell take it, woman, will you do as I say!"

"Do not swear at me, sir."

"Indeed, no," said the Prince as he entered, bearing a glass of wine. "What a pity the infernal quack denied you a drink! This claret is amazingly good. A servant is negotiating to buy the remaining bottles." He drank deeply. "Now, my lord, you must do as you are bid."

"Please, sir, will you not command Miss Wells to return to London? Her good name . . ."

". . . need in no way suffer," interrupted the Prince. "You need her help, and my advice is that neither of you should appear in public after tonight until the Reception at Carlton House at the end of next week. You will be well by then, Verax, and the announcement may be made in my presence. Indeed, I should like that very much."

"Announcement?" Cassandra almost gaped.

"Of your betrothal. It will silence all tattle-mongers. I daresay you and Verax were not intending to make the happy news public so soon, but your hands have been forced by that villain, Pierce."

"But, sir," protested Cassandra in anguish.

"Do not thank me," wheezed the Prince genially. "Promise me only that you will say nothing to anyone – not even your gracious chaperone! So gratifying for your Prince to be the first with such glad news."

"Sir, I . . ."

"So very romantic of Verax to drive into the night to save you." Ready moisture sprang to the Prince's eyes. "I recall the time when I . . . well, no matter." He finished his wine. "Now I am going on to London. I shall relish the next few days as I listen to the tabbycats and their evil mutterings, knowing that they will be confounded at my Reception."

Why did not Verax speak? Cassandra looked at him then forgot everything as she saw his hectic complexion. In his weakness and agitation his endeavours to articulate were useless, and with a final word of encouragement the Prince left.

Problems were forgotten as Verax's fever mounted and he resisted all Daniel's efforts to give him medicine until Cassandra took the spoonful of syrup and held it to his mouth. "Drink this and don't be such a crosspatch," she ordered.

Startled by this resurgence of nursery language the Marquis opened his mouth and Cassandra poured in the syrup which he gulped down.

When he slept she wrote an explanatory letter to Lady Alethea, and a footman was sent to London. Cassandra shared the nursing with Eliza and Daniel and was alarmed as the fever increased. The apothecary pronounced that it must run its course, and that his lordship must not be moved for at least a week.

Verax's eyes followed Cassandra about the room. "I am troubled to think of the stories which must be circulating London," he said.

Cassandra tried to shrug, but they were not surprised when the footman brought a letter from Lady Alethea, penned in great agitation, saying that rumour had it that Miss Wells was residing in the house of Sir Vincent Pierce, who was also out of town. "For heaven's sake, return and give them the lie," she begged.

Verax groaned. "That man knows how to ruin a reputation."

The letter continued, "I have heard that Susan is safe in Oxford and Hugh's mother is with her, and I have sent Bella, so all your trouble was for nothing."

Cassandra fumed. She had tumbled into Sir Vincent's trap and could see no future but to return to Ridgefield. Verax was watching her closely. "It seems that the Prince has arrived at the only solution."

Colour ran up under her skin. "Never! I will not be driven to the arms of a man!"

"Of course not," he soothed, "but we may be betrothed."

"No! Such a contract is binding."

"We must silence the scurrilous lies."

"I will not agree! I will go abroad."

"You will run away? At some time you must return."

She was silent, twisting the fringe of her shawl. "I wish I had never come to London."

"You cannot wish the past away."

The words hung between them, reminding her of the hurt she had given him.

He said, "You enjoy society. You cannot want to be for ever cut off from it. If you do not follow the Prince's plan he will be exceedingly angry. Furthermore he will think badly of us both, as will everyone."

"He has no right to assume we are in love!"

"Nevertheless he took it for granted that I should not have followed you had I not cared for you."

Again they were silent, and Cassandra ventured a look at the Marquis. He lay back, watching her through narrowed lids, his face pale and lined with pain. She was almost overwhelmed by her love for him and she searched his face for some sign which might indicate that she could win his love if she tried.

She sat down heavily by his bed and he reached out and took her hand. It required all her will not to press her lips to his fingers, not to implore him to find a spark of the love she had destroyed.

"Don't look so desperate, Cassandra," he said, almost briskly. "I will be kind to you."

He moved his thumb gently over the back of her hand and her love and longing engulfed her. She heard a voice which sounded unlike hers agreeing to a betrothal – of convenience only.

In a week Verax was well enough to move, and the party returned to London, where Daniel escorted Cassandra and Eliza home, his master having obeyed the apothecary's instruction to go straight to his bed for a rest.

Cassandra was pounced upon by Lady Alethea. "What are we to do about the dreadful stories? I have told everyone until I was blue-faced that you went on a visit, and chanced upon Lord Verax taken ill at an inn and kindly agreed to supervise his nursing, but no one believes me."

"Hardly surprising," retorted Cassandra, "since it is not true."

Lady Alethea gave her a fulminating look. "You would not credit the stares and sniggers I have seen! The Patronesses have intimated that the Almack's vouchers may not be forthcoming – and the questions I have been asked about Susan! I keep saying she is in Oxford with friends, but it all looks so singular."

She sank on to a couch and waved her hartshorn beneath her nose. "I am not used to such alarms."

"Nor am I," sighed Cassandra. "Later we will talk, but just now I long only for a bath and a change of clothes. I am still wearing the gown in which I left London, and I shall tell Eliza to get rid of it."

Bathing before a fire in warm scented water, Cassandra could have relaxed if she had not been engaged in trying to placate Nurse. Her fury at Eliza's air of smug secrecy was unendurable, but it was evident that she would not easily be pacified. Cassandra could only hope that the news about to break would take her mind from her indignation.

The day of the Carlton House Reception arrived. Recalling the lavish use of colour by the Prince, Cassandra wore cream satin with Mechlin lace, pearls, eardrops and necklace. Susan, who had returned from Oxford with a new look of gravity, was persuaded into white silk and gauze and her most modest diamonds. Even Lady Alethea contented herself with amber brocade, and their carriage joined the others in the crawl along the pillared front of the Regent's residence, while sightseers peered into the coaches and made audible remarks about their occupants.

Susan gasped at the heat inside Carlton House, and they waited in the crowded reception chamber until the Prince was ready to enter.

Verax joined them and Cassandra could not meet his eyes as he rose from his bow. In her sudden panic she might have fled, but His Highness came into the room.

Lady Alethea smothered a gasp. "He has grown even larger," she murmured behind her fan. "Whatever became of the young Prince Florizel?"

Verax bent to Cassandra's ear. "No doubt he is inside wishing he could emerge," he breathed.

In spite of her agitation Cassandra's lips quivered, and she implored him not to make her laugh. She was immensely relieved she had kept her composure, when the Prince scarcely paused with the more consequential guests before making for her.

"Miss Wells, how delightful to see you at our trifling amusement."

Susan's face was suffused with blushes when she was introduced and the Prince complimented Lady Alethea on the beauty of her charges, then he spoke to Lord Verax. "You are welcome, sir. We wish to hear a full account of the fighting in Spain and how you sustained your wound."

His eyes twinkled in conspiratorial pleasure as he moved away and Verax muttered, "I told him everything on our journey to Sittingbourne. He is playing his part to the full."

"Oh, God, I wish the evening was ended," said Cassandra. "When will he make the announcement, I wonder?"

She saw the looks which were directed her way. She could not avoid seeing the eyes above many fans while the ladies made it insultingly obvious that their lips were busy dripping venomous gossip.

"Do you think the Prince has forgotten?" she implored Verax.

The Marquis's brows rose. "My dear Cassandra! Are you so eager for our union to be known? I had believed you reluctant."

She threw him a fulminating look, her feelings so lacerated that she could not summon up a retort. Her lingering hope of breaking free was shattered. She could not continue to inhabit a society which thought her wanton, yet her nerves shrank from a public pretence of love for a man who was simply helping her from a disastrous situation.

When Verax was called to the Prince's side she braced herself for a summons. None came. His Royal Highness led his group away and Lady Alethea, Susan and Cassandra went to the Rose Satin Drawing Room, which was not so crowded. They crossed the expanse of turquoise and gold carpet and sat on a couch in front of a window draped in pink.

"I knew we should not have come," groaned Lady Alethea behind her fan.

"What ails you, ma'am?" asked Susan, surprised. "Now that Mama has said I may wait for Hugh we can easily confound my critics. I was rash, I admit, but came to no harm in Oxford."

Lady Alethea looked at her almost without comprehension. "What? Oh, yes, of course. I am not referring to your escapade."

"Then what . . . ?"

"Cousin Alethea," interrupted Cassandra, "Susan knows nothing . . ."

"What has happened?" Susan's clear young voice trilled through a void in the talk and several people stopped everything to stare.

Her ladyship nudged Cassandra. "There is Lady Birch – the most mischievous tongue in England." She nodded a greeting which set her feathered headdress dancing.

Lady Birch lifted an eyeglass. "It *is* you, Lady Alethea, *and* Miss Wells and Miss Susan Wells. Rumour had it that the two young ladies were out of town."

"Rumour," retorted Lady Alethea with dignity, "is seldom correct."

She managed to insinuate that Lady Birch was as unreliable a source of truth as rumour, and that dame breathed heavily, her emerald and diamond brooches rising and falling like craft upon a peacock satin ocean. She turned to her companion, a thin woman in a crimson gown and a headdress of red and orange petals, and said in a stage-whisper, "When I see Sir Thomas I shall give him the lie direct. He was so sure!"

Since she had not addressed Lady Alethea it was more than the affronted lady could do to ignore etiquette enough to answer. She said angrily to Cassandra, "I knew how it would be. Depend upon it, we shall be for ever having to ward off such evil-minded people."

The woman in red remarked to Lady Birch, "I had it from Lord Quentin Strang that the gentlemen came back to town in a quake of mirth at Sir Vincent's success in hoaxing – a certain person."

"What do they mean?" said Susan.

"If by *they*," answered her ladyship, "you are referring to the creature in the blue dress, and the one who looks like an animated begonia, they are – *persons* – who appear to have been bamboozled by men of their acquaintance."

Since she had spoken only to her immediate companions the two women opposite feigned not to have heard, though their looks should have taken the curl from her ladyship's feathers.

Cassandra was fanning herself as heat and embarrassment and anger reddened her face when a remark by Susan electrified the entire company. "There is Sir Vincent," she cried with pleasure.

Cassandra had to remind herself that Susan was ignorant of the events in Sittingbourne, and before anyone could stop her she had lifted her hand in a salute and, watched by everyone in the room, the baronet strolled towards them.

He looked down at them for a moment and even Susan's spirits were dampened by the expression in his glittering eyes, before he smiled thinly. "Servant, Lady Alethea – Miss Wells – Miss Susan."

Cassandra looked into his lined face, trying to ignore the barely healed cut on his cheek. It was still visible in spite of heavily applied powder and paint. She despised his effrontery in approaching a woman he had so insulted. Lady Alethea stirred restlessly.

Voices around them had begun to whisper in a sibilant murmur as Susan asked suddenly, "Have you sustained an accident, Sir Vincent?"

Instantly there was silence. The baronet fingered his cheek. "A mere trifle, ma'am. My fool of a servant slipped while shaving me."

"H . . . how careless of him," stammered Susan. Even she was aware that so serious a cut could not have come from a clumsy shave.

"Was it not? I shall not forget it, for I think I will always bear a scar."

His eyes flickered towards Cassandra, who silently willed her cousin to leave the room, but her ladyship was in a stubborn mood which determined her to out-sit Lady Birch and her friend. Susan, bewildered by the antagonism surrounding them stammered, "I . . . I have some happy news, Sir Vincent."

The baronet raised his brows, "Indeed?"

"Y . . . yes, sir. I am to be permitted to wait for a betrothal to my dear Hugh."

At Lady Alethea's scandalised protest Susan said defensively, "Well, Sir Vincent was good enough to listen to my worries. He deserves to know the happy outcome."

Lady Alethea's answer was forestalled by Sir Vincent, who said in a barely audible voice, "I have heard that yours is not the only attachment in the family."

"What? What does he mean?" demanded Lady Alethea. "What do you mean, sir?"

Her outrage had overcome her caution, and once more the room was still as Sir Vincent said, "A rumour reached me that Miss Cassandra Wells and a certain friend from her past will be joined in a happy state."

All eyes turned to Cassandra who felt her face flame in blushes. She fanned herself. "It is astonishing how folk are ready to listen to tattlemongers."

"In this case the source was a noble one, madam."

Cassandra maintained an outward calm. She

stared into Sir Vincent's malevolent eyes. Was he
speaking from sheer malice, attempting to push her
into an intolerable situation? Or had the Prince's
eagerness to impart news preceded tonight's
announcement?

As an unmistakable voice was heard from the corridor the guests rose quickly, and Sir Vincent stepped to one side of the couch. All eyes turned to the
double doors as the Prince Regent, with members of
his coterie, entered engaged in conversation with
Lord Verax.

"And you say, my dear sir, that Sir Everard's skill
saved your life? And Sir William Knighton forbade
you to soldier again. Well, you must listen to him.
He has my full confidence." He sighed. "How gladly
would I join our fighting men! That is so, is it not,
Alvanley? Sefton?"

Their lordships agreed, and the Prince looked
about him with his sweet smile. "Do not stand on
ceremony. Be seated, dear ladies, and resume your
conversation. I daresay you were discussing some
bon mot, eh?"

Sir Vincent's voice cut across the buzz of talk. "I
was about to congratulate Miss Wells on her happiness, sir."

The Prince's eyes bulged slightly as he stared at
Cassandra who rose. "Sir Vincent speaks only of his
. . . speculation . . . of rumour."

"Which came from a . . . a substantial source,"
persisted Sir Vincent.

"Indeed! And will you be good enough to share
this morsel with us," demanded the Prince.

Sir Vincent paled beneath his maquillage. "I was
reliably informed that Miss Wells was to be bet-

rothed to Lord Verax. I am surprised he has not already informed you."

Cassandra watched the Prince as many expressions flitted over his face. Clearly he was angry at being denied the pleasure of announcing his news. He motioned Cassandra to him. "Have you spoken to anyone on the matter?"

"Indeed, not, sir."

"And you, Lord Verax, have you discussed the subject in question with anyone?"

"I have not, sir."

"I see." The room was silent as the Prince wrestled with his disappointment, then he smiled delightedly. "The world is not so up-to-the-minute as it likes to think." He took Cassandra's hand and joined it to Verax's. "I myself have the pleasure of telling you that these two dear subjects of His Majesty have reached the sublime culmination of their years of friendship, and your felicitations are in order. They are to be married."

Cassandra suppressed her gasp as she felt the tremor which ran through Jonathan, and knew his shock to be as great as hers. In his determination to be first the Prince had forced them into a situation where it was certain that someone would ask the date of the ceremony.

CHAPTER
TEN

CASSANDRA had not anticipated that the questioner would be Sir Vincent. He risked a public snub by saying smoothly, "Can Your Royal Highness tell us the date of the happy occasion?"

The Prince gave no sign that he had heard, but continued to address the company. "Once such an announcement is made the wedding will not be delayed, especially since these two good people have waited so long. Wedded bliss is, to me, the most desirable state in the world."

Everyone was silent as they contemplated the disastrous marriage of the Prince to Caroline of Brunswick.

Sir Vincent persisted, "Your loyal subjects know how you revere the married state, sir, and we are anxious to learn the date of Lord Verax's marriage to Miss Wells."

There was a further silence during which the Regent permitted himself one baleful glance at Sir Vincent. Verax raised Cassandra's hand and his lips touched her fingers briefly before he released her.

The Prince spoke to Lady Alethea. "How say you, ma'am? There is nothing to delay the ceremony, is there?"

She answered with an inarticulate murmur and he continued, "The Allied armies must soon be in

Paris. Lady Alethea, you must arrange matters quickly, and the bride-trip can be spent partly in that delightful city. They can set the fashion again."

His smile grew more expansive. "I have a capital notion. You shall give an evening entertainment after the wedding – a dinner party. Nothing elaborate, of course – and I shall attend it."

He left the room and Cassandra sank on to a couch. She saw the malignant satisfaction on Sir Vincent's face and knew that he had gauged her perfectly. He had precipitated her into a situation out of which she and Verax could not escape without a public scandal.

Lady Birch and her friend hurried to Lady Alethea. "What a singular honour," they breathed. "How delightful for you all."

Lady Alethea swelled in triumph as she nodded in a manner in which dignity was nicely blended with rejection and the ladies, seeing that their admittedly faint hope of being invited to what must surely be the wedding of the year was non-existent, hurried from the room.

"Oh, no," moaned Cassandra, holding her hot face, "in minutes everyone will know. Oh, God, what am I to do?"

"Do?" demanded her ladyship. "You can congratulate yourself on gaining a distinction for which most women would give their teeth! And we must begin at once to plan your gown and the celebration." She peered at Lord Verax. "You say nothing, sir, but I daresay you are overcome. And you are not well yet. Better return home and go to bed with a hot posset. You must be strong for the great day."

Verax was staring over her head and she realised

that Sir Vincent was leaning on the wall, an interested spectator. Something in the Marquis's eyes caused him to stand upright and stroll forward. Then his white hand touched his scarred face, and he bowed and left.

Lady Alethea said to Cassandra, "I would have expected you to tell me first about a betrothal. Does your brother know?"

When Cassandra shook her head her ladyship tried to produce a disapproving expression, but she could not keep it up. "To think I shall have the honour of entertaining the Prince," she crowed. She looked at Susan. "Close your mouth! You gape like a country wench!"

"As well she might," muttered Cassandra to Verax as he bent over her solicitously.

His lips twitched as he held out his arm. "Will you walk with me in the Conservatory, dearest? You are flushed."

"She is overset by joy," said Lady Alethea.

Even the enormous Gothic Conservatory was hot, but since Cassandra's agitation sprang from her emotions the temperature did not impress her. Other couples strolled on the square-tiled floor beneath the arched roof with pillared supports, where a flirtation could be enjoyed without eavesdroppers.

"How are we to escape from this dreadful trap?" demanded Cassandra.

Verax placed his hand over hers and his touch scorched through her glove. "Cassie, we are observed," he warned.

More people were entering, their eyes turning repeatedly to the couple whom the Prince had honoured in an almost unprecedented way.

Cassandra forced a smile. "Jonathan, you must find a way out. You know we are not to be married."

She lowered her voice as her eye was caught by a lady she had met only once before. "Good heavens, there is her Grace of Riverbridge! She scarcely deigned to acknowledge my existence and now she is bowing and smiling."

"Then bow and smile also, my future bride."

Cassandra obeyed, saying through gritted teeth, "I am no such thing!"

"Well, everyone believes you so and they are closing in on us. Imagine the consequence attached to those who are at the wedding feast."

"They will be few!" exclaimed Cassandra. "That is to say, there will be no one, for there will be no feast. Why must you torment me?"

"Please try to look happy. I am simply endeavouring to amuse you. It will damage my reputation considerably if you act as if you were about to be dragged to your execution."

Cassandra summoned up a smile. "Well, tonight I will play a part, but tomorrow we must devise a plan of escape."

Then appeared ladies who struck apprehension into braver hearts than Cassandra's. Lady Castlereagh and Mrs. Drummond Burrell, those *grandes dames* of London society, surveyed the pair with mesmeric stares as they offered their congratulations.

"We have heard," announced Mrs. Drummond Burrell, "that His Highness is to grace your nuptials. You will have many persons soliciting invitations. His Highness must never be subjected to vulgar company at a private gathering."

"Indeed, he must not," agreed Verax blandly.

"However, there are those who must receive invitations," continued Mrs. Drummond Burrell inexorably.

Lady Castlereagh gave a grave nod and they looked expectantly at Verax until he murmured, "You may rest assured that the leading members of the *ton* will not be left out."

They directed approving smiles at the couple before moving on their stately way.

"What are you about?" Cassandra breathed in horror. "You have promised them that they will attend a function which will never take place."

Verax did not answer, but guided her expertly through the converging company back into the largest reception room which was so chokingly hot that the painted faces were beginning to dissolve, feathers were wilting and half-fainting women were semi-recumbent on sofas. There was an air of excitement which proved to be arising from a report that the Prince Regent had sent an order to Sir Vincent Pierce to remove himself from Carlton House.

"He has ruined himself," said Verax. "The Prince will never forget, or forgive, Pierce's insolence."

Cassandra's fuming anger was not abated by the news, and she watched helplessly as Lady Alethea and a delighted Susan enjoyed their position as centre of attention, the chief protagonists in the drama having proved disappointingly reticent. Cassandra asked bitterly, "What possesses you to continue this farce? I shall be utterly sunk when the truth is known. I had as well resign myself to following Pierce into the low echelons of society."

"My dear," said Verax in exaggerated astonishment, "if you feel like that why did you allow me to rescue you from him?"

Cassandra turned to rend him with a retort, but as she looked into her tormentor's laughing eyes she caught her breath. Her longing to hold him close, to hear him say that their marriage was what he wanted above all else, overwhelmed her. She put out a shaking hand. "I cannot endure any more."

Instantly he was grave, and steered her through the crowd to a quiet alcove where he sent for iced champagne. As Cassandra sipped he called a senior footman.

"Pray take this message to His Royal Highness. Lord Verax and Miss Wells present their humble duty and wish to convey their regret that they must leave Carlton House. Miss Wells is suffering from an indisposition precipitated by the singular mark of esteem done her by her Prince."

Cassandra was on her second glass of wine and she felt an inelegant giggle bubbling up. "He will never remember all that!"

"Indeed I shall, ma'am," said the footman haughtily. "I have an excellent memory."

They watched his splendid silk-covered calves and powdered wig disappear down the corridor, and Cassandra felt suddenly weary. She was glad when Verax escorted her to his carriage and wished her goodnight at the door of the Park Lane house. "Tomorrow I will call, Cassie," he murmured, kissing her hand. "I left word with Lady Alethea that we were leaving."

In spite of her weariness Cassandra could not sleep properly, and she suffered dreams in which

Jonathan's face mingled with Sir Vincent's, and she found herself at an altar rail with the Prince Regent while Princess Caroline screamed insults from the doorway.

When she heard the others return in the early hours she sat up and lighted her candle then went to watch the dawn lightening the sky. Could it be only three months since she had discovered Susan eloping with Hugh? And now the impulsive Susan had gained her heart's desire while she, the so-called Crystal Venus, had become embroiled in a harrowing situation with the man whose love for her she had killed so long ago.

She rose early and sat alone in the morning room, riffling the pages of a magazine as she waited for Lord Verax. He was with her quite soon and she sprang to her feet. "Jonathan! I was afraid you would sleep half the day."

He took her hands. "How cold you are! And so pale and fatigued." He led her to a chair near the fire. "I have been used to keeping early hours. You will grow accustomed to my ways."

"Verax! Do not jest! You know we are not to be married."

He gave her an unfathomable look then to her stupefaction went down on one knee. "Miss Wells, it cannot have escaped your notice that I have long admired you." He laid a hand on his heart. "Will you do me the honour of becoming my wife?" He rose, dusting his knees. "There, was not that proper? These matters should be well conducted."

She gave a laugh which was half a sob. "Your playacting alters nothing. What are we to do?"

"My offer is made in all seriousness."

She drew a breath to argue, then her knees went weak at his smile. "Would marriage to me be so bad?" he asked.

"No! Yes! Oh, you are confusing me. I want to be your friend always – but *I* do not wish to be wed – to anyone."

She had risen and now stared into his dark eyes. He stroked her soft cheek with one finger. "How beautiful you are. What a pity if it were all wasted."

Cassandra fought her desire to lean against him as she flashed, "Which it would be, I suppose, if not lavished on some vain male!"

He grinned. "Your eyes sparkle wonderfully when you are angry. I must hope that we disagree sometimes when we are wed."

She stepped back from him, her body shaken by an uncontrollable mixture of emotions. With all the power of her passionate nature, long denied, she wanted him, but something – pride – fear – held her fast. When he suggested they sit together on a couch she had no will to resist.

He spoke quietly. "Already this morning I have been visited by one of the Prince's secretaries, bearing a note affirming that His Highness will attend our wedding feast and requesting the date. Are we to tell him that his magnificent gesture made in public was engendered by falseness? He would be driven into one of his frenzies. He would see another opportunity for the satirists to lampoon him."

"Am I to be sacrificed to the Prince's dignity?"

"No, indeed not, Cassandra. But do not forget that all this was begun to save your name. Any hint that we are not betrothed and your reputation will be in shreds."

"A betrothal is not a marriage! A betrothal can be broken!"

"Not by me!" His grim tone startled her. "You may be prepared to flout society's rules then bury yourself in the country, but I am not. I have been a serving soldier and need a stimulating life. I may enter politics, and for that I need an unblemished past."

Her body tautened and then went limp: she owed Jonathan heavy debts. She spoke through lips which could scarcely form the words. "I cannot fight you all. Let it be. A marriage of convenience – let it be that."

"Splendid!" He kissed her hand briefly. Now that he had gained his way he became brisk and unemotional. She tried to read his thoughts in his eyes, but they were impersonal as he left, saying he must begin making arrangements.

Lady Alethea took over the wedding. At one moment she was in transports of delight, the next in deep despair. Cassandra's ivory silk slip, to be worn beneath a Venetian lace overdress, was an inch too long and must be returned to the dressmaker. The size of the dinner service must be increased and London was combed for matching dishes. The question of the meal vexed her to distraction.

"Surely, ma'am," protested Susan, "the Prince does not expect four removes and a choice of twelve soups."

"Much you know!" screamed her ladyship. "He sits down to dinners far larger and thinks it all ordinary."

Lord Verax produced from his cellars a magnificent choice of wines which were handed to a reverent butler to guard, while Nurse and Eliza vied in so ferocious a manner that Cassandra arrived at her wedding day with her strained nerves stretched to their utmost endurance.

When she was ready she dismissed her maids, the dressmakers and the French hairdresser and stared at her reflection in the cheval-glass. She touched the beautiful diamond and pearl parure which was a Verax heirloom. She had never looked lovelier, nor felt more frightened.

Lady Alethea entered. "How pretty you are! But you are pale. Though that is proper in a lady about to wed. The carriage is at the door and your brother-in-law waits downstairs to give you his escort."

Cassandra felt a surge of longing for her sister who was unwell, and a stab of terror when she thought of the reason. Lady Alethea misinterpreted her expression. "You have no need to be nervous. The ceremony will be simple and the dinner party distinguished." Pleasure lit her face as she remembered the past scores she had been able to repay with interest as she dispensed, or withheld, invitations. Cassandra remained still and her ladyship said impatiently, "Come, my dear. We must go. You are not going to faint, are you?"

Cassandra looked at her cousin. "I . . . I do not think . . . I am sure . . . that is to say, Lord Verax does not love me."

Lady Alethea's tall, feathered and flowered headdress shook. "Does not love you? What has that to do with anything? People of our rank leave that kind of thing to the vulgar. Sir Ralph and I did very well together, and the absence of maudlin sentimentality enabled me to bear his demise with composure. You are not to be influenced by some romantic novel, are you?"

"No, of course not!"

"There then! You are full of sensibility, but soon you will be settled. Only think of your future rank and fortune!"

It was astonishing how many fashionable folk found important business in Hanover Square that morning as Cassandra left St. George's Church on her husband's arm. The ceremony had seemed unreal, as did the remainder of the day. His Highness praised the dinner and tucked an amazing quantity of food and drink into his portly frame, over which his elegant jacket was stretched.

The guests numbered thirty – "a delightfully intimate party", approved the Prince as he toasted the couple and prepared to leave them "to enjoy one another".

Cassandra swept him a deep curtsy and he held out his hand for her kiss. "Lady Verax, you are a truly lovely bride. I am sure that Her Majesty will be enchanted with you when you attend her Drawing Room as a married lady."

His words almost made Cassandra topple. She had forgotten the necessity for a second presentation as a newly wed woman, and her idea of spending the remainder of the Season in seclusion to escape the sharp-eyed gossips must be set aside.

That night as Eliza brushed her mistress's hair Nurse admitted Lord Verax to the bedchamber. Both maids left instantly, and Cassandra stared at the closed door as if mesmerised by the shock of becoming abruptly aware of his right to enter her apartments.

He spoke softly. "Do you fear to look at me?"

Slowly she turned her head and met the dark eyes in which lurked an unfathomable expression. He seemed to be searching for something in her face as he took her hand. At his touch she found it needful to summon all her control to prevent the trembling of her body. For a long moment they remained motionless, before the Marquis bent to brush her fingers with his lips.

"You were an exquisite bride, my dear."

Then he turned and left, and as he went Cassandra was assailed by a torrent of sensations. She was relieved and disappointed by his departure. She wished he had paid her further compliments. She railed at her own foolishness. Her husband was too experienced to talk in intimacy to a woman for whom he had no desire.

She lay in her chaste bed and ached with yearning for his arms about her, the passion of his lips on hers. Then all was swept aside in memories of her mother who had died so young and of her sister preparing yet again to face the dangers of childbed. She rebelled against a fate which had thrown her into a bond in which her love warred with unnatural horror.

She thought she would not sleep, but her tired body won and the morning found her determined to keep this mock-marriage upon a footing which would ensure her future tranquillity.

She was driven to the Marquis's imposing mansion in Berkeley Square and installed in rooms so richly furnished that even Nurse was overawed. At any other time Cassandra would have been amused by her Ancient Retainer's open-mouthed amazement, but now she was too preoccupied by the

belated realisation that Verax had not actually agreed
in words that their marriage would be one of convenience only. Would he continue to respect her
wishes? Had his forbearance last night been a gesture
to her weariness?

When Verax paid her his second visit simply to
wish her goodnight she watched the door close
behind him and could not decide which emotion was
uppermost. The suppressed need of a woman in
love, or the determination of the cool bride who
demanded her virginal bed.

It seemed that her husband did not need her
embraces, and that even in private she must show
him cool courtesy while falling deeper in love with a
man who combined intense personal magnetism
with gallantry and compassion.

For her first public appearance as a wife Cassandra
wore a draped Florentine blue tunic in Persian silk,
and Eliza coiled her thick gold hair into a Grecian
style, securing it with combs of lapis lazuli which
were one of Verax's gifts to his bride. She dusted her
cheeks with pink Spanish paper. Not for worlds
would she allow the sharp-eyed dames a chance to
gossip. Her husband was awaiting her at the foot of
the stairs and she shivered as his eyes rested for a
fraction of a second on her sapphires, the ones she
had worn on that unhappy night in Clifton.

His severe black and white garb, a gold fob at his
waist and an emerald pin in his faultless cravat, was
an austere outfit which suited to perfection his athletic body and lean features.

They were silent on the drive to the Jersey residence, where they met Lady Alethea and Susan.
Verax bent over her ladyship's hand. "How magnifi-

cent you look," he murmured, causing Cassandra to emit a choked laugh.

Her cousin was gowned with a splendour she considered fitting for a lady whose relative had captured the Season's biggest marriage prize, and Cassandra followed the expanse of Medici crimson velvet, topped by a turban of pink feathers, as they climbed the stairs to the reception party. It was easier to concentrate on her cousin's appearance than to wonder if she had imagined that Verax's eyes had lingered on Susan.

When he had learned of her love for Hugh he had made no sign of being hurt. The news had left him free to marry Cassandra. Had Susan the power to keep her husband from desiring her? She was shaken by a wave of jealousy.

The Countess of Jersey greeted them with a trill of laughter. "I congratulate you, Jonathan, on having won the hand of a lady so difficult to please." Her malice was tempered by a smile. "My felicitations, Lady Verax. The conviction that you have disappointed so many fond mamas and eager young ladies can only add to your joy."

Cassandra curtsied, biting back a retort. She would have to thicken her skin, for there would be abundant talk about a woman of her age having snatched the handsome and wealthy Marquis from beneath the noses of the latest crop of marriageable girls. There must be plenty of speculation as to how she had achieved it. No doubt Sir Vincent's friends had been busy!

CHAPTER
ELEVEN

In the main reception room they were accosted by an elderly man with a painted face and high-heeled shoes with enormous silver buckles. He bowed with a flourish as he said, "Good evening, my lord – and Lady Verax also. How charming you look, my lady. You have been out of town, have you not – you and the fair Miss Susan? And you too, my lord, were sadly missed. Were they not missed, Quentin?"

Lord Quentin Strang tittered. "Yes, indeed! And such odd stories were circulating. Was it your health again, my lord?"

Verax bowed. "So good of you to concern yourself, Strang."

Lord Quentin wafted a scented, lace-trimmed handkerchief. "Not at all, my dear fellow. But I am glad to know that the torments which we less fortunate males have suffered at the hands of the cool Miss Wells are now assuaged for you."

His words unleashed a dam, and the party was assailed and congratulations were said and questions asked. Verax countered them while steering the ladies through the throng into the supper room. They sipped champagne while Verax took claret.

Susan looked nervous. "They were like birds of prey. Is society always like that?"

"Yes," replied Cassandra shortly. "That is why

we have endeavoured to keep you from scandalising it."

"But what about you?" cried Susan. "You went at once to Lord Verax – at an inn too – when he was ill."

Cassandra opened and closed her mouth. Susan had been given part of the truth and could not be blamed for being puzzled.

Lord Verax spoke smoothly. "Your Aunt Cassandra's heart was permitted to rule her head on that occasion. And you must remember, Susan, that what might be considered indecorous in a young lady can be allowed in a lady of your aunt's years."

"I see," faltered Susan. "But those people were hinting that Aunt Cassandra had behaved with . . . impropriety."

Verax's sigh was exaggerated. "Once the tabbies get hold of a tale they make it truly scurrilous."

Cassandra gave a gracious smile to a passing duchess whose eyes devoured her as she brought a halt to this infuriating exchange. "Pray, Jonathan, bring me a morsel of chicken. I vow I am quite hungry."

He raised his brows humorously but obeyed, and she was forced to swallow food for which she had no need.

When they returned to the reception room Cassandra saw a man who made her stumble. Standing in a corner, surrounded by dandies, stood Sir Thomas Aldred. A burst of laughter came from them before someone noticed Lord Verax and nudged Sir Thomas. In one of those inexplicable lulls his voice could be heard declaiming, "There she is! Vincent was as mad as fire to lose her!" Then, realising that his voice had carried, he pretended to examine his fingernails.

Lord Verax held a gentle but firm hand beneath his wife's elbow and propelled her through the crowd. He made no obvious haste, stopping to greet well-wishers, but steered Cassandra inexorably to the side of Sir Thomas, who seemed to have been turned to stone.

Verax bowed. "Good evening. I believe you mentioned Sir Vincent. How is our noble baronet?"

Sir Thomas stuttered. "He . . . he is . . . is perfectly well, sir. That is to say, he has suffered a slight . . . slight indisposition. What I mean is that his friends hope to see him again quite soon."

"Ah! He has left London?"

"F . . . for a while, sir."

"I see. Perhaps you heard that I was in the country – for a while. I was taken by a fever, the result of my wound sustained in Spain. This lady, who has honoured me with her hand in marriage, came at once to my help." Verax lifted Cassandra's hand and brushed her kid glove lightly with his lips, though he did not take his eyes from Sir Thomas. "I should have expected no other from my dearest betrothed, Sir Thomas. She nursed me and I recovered quickly. Was not that clever of her?"

"Oh, yes, indeed it was." The sweating knight pulled out a handkerchief and mopped his brow.

"You find it warm, sir," enquired Verax in solicitous tones. "I had forgotten how hot the London houses can be. When one is fighting Britain's enemies one endures much discomfort. But there are compensations. So much opportunity to practice the martial arts."

"I am sure you are right, sir."

"Oh, yes, I am right. I am an expert with weapons, Sir Thomas."

Verax's hand slid down his eyeglass and he surveyed the knight and his friends. "I am convinced that only a lapse in your memories has prevented you from wishing all happiness and a peaceful life to my wife and myself, gentlemen."

Their congratulations were lavish and profuse before Lord Verax took his wife back to Lady Alethea, who had sunk upon a rout-chair and was being fanned vigorously by Susan while assuring her that the men had been indulging in spiteful gossip about her aunt's nursing Lord Verax at an inn.

She raised a limp hand. "Do not disturb the air so violently, Susan. You will ruin my coiffure. Oh, I thought I should die of mortification," she hissed.

"My . . . husband is capable of dealing with any situation," retorted Cassandra. She had paused, not only remembering the time when Jonathan Verax could only blush and stammer when faced with malicious cruelty, but realising that she found the new word unexpectedly sweet.

Lady Jersey had been a delighted witness, and now she drifted over. "Vouchers for Almack's will arrive for you tomorrow," she promised. She smiled into Lord Verax's eyes. "Well done, sir. London will be more amusing for your presence."

As she left Lady Alethea nodded in triumph. "Well, that is a hurdle cleared!"

She then gave her gracious consent to an unexceptionable young Viscount to escort Susan to a room where a dance was being got up, while Cassandra fumed in helpless rage. She had been hurried into marriage because a foolish girl had not confided legitimate worries to her guardian! Now, it appeared, she and her husband had been cast in the roles of entertainers to the *ton* world.

The evening left her exhaustedly wondering how she would find the stamina to maintain her farce of a marriage for the rest of the Season.

When she and Verax drove in Hyde Park she smiled at acquaintances until she felt her face was stretched in a permanent grin. "How false it all is!" she burst out, then bit her lip, dreading her husband's reply.

He merely raised his whip to salute a passing carriage and asked, "Tired of me already, Cassandra?"

"Do not be facetious! It is more than I can bear."

Her voice cracked and he looked down at her then pulled the horses to a walk. He covered her hands momentarily with his. "I am sorry if it is all hard on you. It was your selfless attempt to rescue Susan and then your care of me which landed you in such a predicament. What do you find particularly difficult?"

"The awful – pretence!"

Her heart lurched with the word. There was no pretence about her love for Verax.

He was silent as the high-bred greys pulled the light phaeton beneath trees still bare of foliage. Cassandra shivered in the icy breeze and Lord Verax said, "You are cold. It is time we returned home."

Home! The word constricted in her throat. If he showed her one more mark of consideration, if he touched her again, she felt she would break down and pour out her passion for him. But he increased the horses' pace and they returned to Berkeley Square.

At Almack's that night Susan was scathing. "It is so bare here, and the refreshments are positively cheeseparing."

Lady Alethea frowned her to silence and Susan forgot to criticise as she took the floor with a handsome partner as the orchestra, conducted by Mr. Neil Gow of Edinburgh, struck up for a country dance, aptly named, *Drive the Cold Winter Away*.

Verax, looking wonderfully attractive in the required dress of knee-breeches and silk stockings, a black coat tailored to perfection and a white cravat knotted in a style devised by himself, bowed to his wife and solicited her company in the dance.

She experienced the intense delight of taking her place with him in the long line of ladies and gentlemen whirling and circling, crossing and passing in time to the rhythms. As the movements brought her opposite her husband he said spontaneously, "How lovely you look, Cassandra."

Those within earshot exchanged looks which veered between the amused and scandalised while Cassandra, steeling a heart which was melting with pleasure, felt a perverse fury at being shown in public emotions denied her in private.

"Fie, sir!" she cried. "If you pay me compliments for all to hear we shall be labelled romantics."

Her wit won a ripple of laughter from the others, then their steps carried them apart and she was left wishing she had stilled her tongue. From then on he took his mood from her and maintained the polite brevity which etiquette demanded from a married couple.

Cassandra attended the next Drawing Room and made her married obeisance to Queen Charlotte while a delighted Lady Alethea preened in the background.

"Little did I think," she rejoiced to Lord Verax, "that my duties would prove to be so wonderfully satisfying." She peered at Cassandra. "My dear Lady Verax, you must make Eliza put plenty of colour on your face. You look positively unwell."

As Jonathan and Cassandra drove home Cassandra stirred beside her husband in the intimacy of the carriage and sighed.

"Are you not well, my dear?" asked her husband quietly. "Is that why you are pale?"

"No! I am not ill, though I think I may be if . . ." She stopped then resumed, "I have made my Court curtsy. We do not have to remain in London. Could we not visit your estate in Oxfordshire?"

"Anxious to be alone with me?"

His tone mocked her and she replied angrily, "Not at all, my lord. If it pleases you I could go to my own house in Ridgefield."

"It does not please me. I have no wish to become the butt of crude humour when my wife leaves my – bed so soon after our marriage."

"You know perfectly well . . ."

"Oh, I know all about our wedded joy! But the world and his wife do not – nor shall they. If you wish to leave London we will do so together."

When he wished her goodnight Cassandra said, "I do not want to be at outs with you, Jonathan, but I cannot keep up the deceit in public. In the country I could have time to become accustomed to our marriage."

"You can stop the excuses," he said harshly. "We will go."

"Excuses! It is not entirely my fault we are bound in a hateful union."

Verax turned at the door and walked back to her. "Do you have to make your dislike of me so obvious? We could find compensations."

She saw his purpose in his eyes and made a protest which was lost against his lips as he held her in an iron-hard embrace. This was no boy's tender salute, but a man's angry savagery which turned her liquid and rendered her helpless.

She felt herself responding, her mouth moved under his, then abruptly he released her. "It seems to me, madam, that you are not completely devoid of the needs of the flesh."

He left her touching her bruised lips and she climbed into bed and wept herself to sleep.

The journey to Birkwood in Oxfordshire was accomplished smoothly, and Cassandra was able to see how well-treated were travellers who arrived at inns in crested carriages accompanied by a retinue of servants. She could have enjoyed it if her husband had shown her the slightest hint of tenderness. In the best room at the inn she drifted into a troubled sleep in which images tormented her. She saw herself as a wanted wife, living a full existence, loved, desired, possessed. Waking early, her reason told her that Jonathan had kissed her only to prove his mastery over her.

When the coaches bowled along the perfectly-tended main driveway of Birkwood, between an avenue of oak and beech whose branches were showing a pale hint of green leaves, Cassandra was entranced by the first sight of her new dwelling. The mansion had been built in Tudor times and skilfully extended, so that it had grown into a delight of pale rose brickwork and grey stone with a forest of chimneys from which curled plumes of smoke.

"It looks like a real home!" cried Cassandra.

"It is your home, madam," Verax reminded. "Perhaps you recognised it. Maybe we were predestined for each other."

"Do not jest! Our marriage is all make-believe."

He looked as if he might speak, but they stopped, the steps were let down and he was handing her out of the chaise on to a gravelled path.

Enormous studded doors opened as they climbed a flight of stone steps and Lord Verax led his wife into a galleried hall which stretched upwards for three stories to the roof, though Cassandra had no time to gaze as the first of a lengthy line of servants came to greet her.

"Welcome to Birkwood, Lady Verax, on behalf of your domestics. I am Mrs. Shipley, your housekeeper."

As the dignified woman in black introduced the servants right down to a little kitchen maid who tripped over her feet when she tried to curtsy and earned a frown from the head housemaid, Cassandra smilingly acknowledged each one, but the whole thing had begun to seem dreamlike. In these surroundings of a home which was greater and more luxurious than any she had envisaged for herself, amid a throng of people who waited to do her lightest bidding, with her husband beside her, Cassandra was experiencing a dark unhappiness which gnawed at her with increasing insistence, and she realised that, for the first time in her life, she felt unbearably lonely.

Mrs. Shipley and a maid conducted their mistress up the wide oak stairway with its velvety carpet, followed by footmen with luggage, and Cassandra was shown to an apartment in which the austere beauty of the ancient carved furniture was both tempered and enriched by soft cushions and hangings in delicately blended shades of blue and rose.

Mrs. Shipley clasped her hands in pride. "His lordship sent word that we was to prepare the rooms in colours which suited you best. He chose them, and if you'll pardon the liberty, ma'am, I can see his lordship's meaning."

Eliza arrived in a rush with Nurse, who threw the housekeeper a grim look from beneath grey brows, but Mrs. Shipley dropped a curtsy properly suitable to her equal in station and hoped that her ladyship's personal attendants would find all that was needful for their comfort.

Then she left and Eliza took a deep breath. "Well, Miss Cassandra . . . !" A hand went to her mouth and Nurse gave an irritating little smirk at her colleague's lapse. "I should say, Lady Verax," continued Eliza, "this is a fitting setting for your beauty."

Cassandra touched Eliza's hand, then Nurse's. "Thank you for your care of me through the years," she said in a voice almost suspended by tears.

"Oh, ma'am!" cried Eliza. "May you find the joy in your marriage that I did in mine – short though it was."

Emotion fled before the heavily-charged atmosphere generated by Nurse's snorting fury at this reference to her companion's marital experience, and Cassandra wavered between tears and laughter as a tap on the door was followed by the entrance of her husband.

The maids left, and Cassandra felt a fresh surge of regret for what might have been as he treated her with cool reserve.

"Do you like your rooms?"

"Th . . . this is lovely. I have not seen another."

He walked to a connecting door and opened it and she hurried through to find herself in a bedchamber which was larger than her boudoir and furnished in the same combination of colours in equally delicate taste. The chief difference lay in the enormous four-poster bed which dominated the room.

She glanced at it. "This – is also delightful, my lord."

Verax stared at her with an enigmatic expression then he nodded. "Rest if you like. I must see my steward."

"I would not detain you for the world."

"You make that abundantly clear, madam."

He left her with a low bow, and Cassandra saw in the cheval-glass that her eyes were dilated. She could not rest and Mrs. Shipley took her on a tour of the principal rooms, relating the history of the house and its occupants. "And if you'll pardon the liberty, madam, your ladyship's husband is a sight more to our taste than his late lordship, who was unmindful of his duties to his people."

The Marquis and his lady dined in the small family dining-room, though it seemed large to Cassandra, who reflected that her whole house would almost have fitted into the ballroom.

Verax had been to visit the incumbent of one of the livings in his patronage. "He is elderly and frail," he said. "If you think that Susan's future husband would like it, and if Hugh is suitable, I will offer him the curacy and then the living. It is a handsome one – and the best within my gift."

And will bring Susan near, Cassandra's wayward thoughts ran on before she castigated herself for thinking so ill of Verax and thanked him for his generosity.

His absence seemed to have induced a gentler frame of mind and he tried to put her at ease in the splendid library and later in the music room where he had ordered the pianoforte tuned for her use. His increasing warmth made her nervous as the time to retire approached, but still she lay alone and as the days passed and he continued to treat her with cool courtesy she began to feel convinced that he was content to accept their marriage as one of form only.

At least, she felt almost sure. Sometimes, as they rode or drove in the park, or sat together in candlelit rooms, it seemed to her that a look of need flickered in Jonathan's expressive eyes and that his rare touch held a caress. She was thrown from one emotion to another as longing for his love warred with her fear of the unknown. In her haste to run from the prying eyes of the *haut ton* she had not considered how often they would be alone. Visits to local houses and entertaining took up little time.

Then came a day when they walked in a walled enclosure in the garden where flowers were making an appearance, and the sun held warmth at last. Daniel came hurrying to them with such a joyful face that Verax exclaimed, "There must be good news from France!"

His servant said exultantly, "Bonaparte has abdicated! He was all for pushing on to Paris, but met his retreating infantry. The tidings were so tardy that Lord Wellington fought another engagement."

The men shook hands with the comradeship which had been forged in the necessities of war, before Daniel hastened to spread the news.

Lord Verax turned to Cassandra, excitement lighting his lean features and dark eyes. He pulled her to him and held her so near that she could feel the heavy beating of his heart. Then he kissed her with a lingering passion fuelled by his elation, and she knew a wild urgency to respond. Their mouths clung and she pressed herself to him, then she began to struggle.

He held her at arm's length, staring at her. His face held puzzlement and anger, before the light faded from his eyes and he released her and bowed. "The war is over, my love," he said coolly. "A man may kiss his wife at such a time – and it seemed for a moment that you also thought so."

She hastened into the house. He followed and ordered wine to be served to all, down to the lowliest kitchen wench, to drink to Britain and the damnation of her enemies.

At dinner Verax drank toasts to Lord Wellington and to the men who had survived the war. He drank deeper ones to the men who had fallen. He drank to the Prince who had prophesied that he and his wife could take a bride-trip to Paris. Cassandra was inspired by his gaiety, and laughed with an easy abandon she had not known since childhood; and when she retired she felt more relaxed than she had for a long while.

After bathing she lay in bed remembering their laughter, smiling in the darkness. Then she heard the door of her bedchamber open quietly and recognised the soft tread of her husband.

CHAPTER
TWELVE

HE pulled aside the draperies around the bed and laid his candle upon a table. He looked unexpectedly young in his burgundy-coloured dressing gown, his hair dishevelled as he ran long fingers through it.

Cassandra sat up in bed, tugging the covers to her chin. "What do you want, Jonathan?"

He smiled, and the pupils of his dark eyes were large. "What does any man want of his wife, my dear?"

"You are drunk, sir!"

"Oh, I do not deny I have drunk deeply, but I resent the imputation that I would need to be intoxicated to make an advance to you."

"Must you make fun of everything? We had a pleasant evening. We indulged freely in wine. It was acceptable in view of the news. You . . . you are overwrought, I daresay."

She had tried to keep her mild words even, but her voice shook with the hammering of her heart.

Lord Verax touched her hair with a gentle finger. "Maybe my relief at the ending of hostilities brought me to your bed sooner than I had anticipated, but at some time our union must be consummated. Why not now?"

She went cold with shock as he sat on the bed and stroked her gold hair which streamed over her shoulders. "How beautiful! At the farmhouse it was braided."

She swayed almost imperceptibly towards him, assailed by such longing that her body shook. His touch, so light, so soft, scorched her. She loved him and she ached to fling aside her reservations and embrace him. He saw something in her eyes which made him catch his breath. He leaned near and slid his arms about her, pressing the back of her head so that she was drawn irresistibly nearer.

"No, please . . ." she gasped. "You have forgotten – our marriage – one of convenience . . ."

He laughed against her mouth. "It suits my convenience very well to make love to my incomparable wife. I have been patient with you, but now I demand the response I have earned."

She tried to push him away, but as his lips closed over hers she forgot everything in her helpless desire and her arms stole round his lean body.

He did not leave her until dawn streaked the sky with red bands and picked out the hard outlines of the furniture, while the candle by her bed burned low and died.

Cassandra slept, awoke, and lay still until Eliza entered with her morning tea. The maid's eyes darted to the indented pillow beside her, then she was alone again, reliving the hours of the night.

She knew with age-old wisdom that he had been gentle with her, drawing from her an abandoned response which filled her with shame. How could she have been so lost to passion as to reveal her love when she knew that a man could make the most intimate caresses without his heart being involved?

She leapt from her bed and paced the room, vow-ing that never again would she give such satisfaction to a man who wanted only her body.

Verax continued to visit his wife's apartments and she fought against her own nature, gaining a savage pleasure in withholding the response he sought.

During the day she ached to breach the barrier she was erecting between them, but at night her determination not to show a sign of love to a man who never once mentioned the word, strengthened her resolve.

He became morose and when he asked her if she would care to join the crowds of English people who were flocking to liberated Paris she agreed with relief. Foreign travel would give them something to discuss. While the maids were packing she walked into the garden, past men who were preparing the ground for the delayed planting.

Verax found her in the shrubbery, where he handed her a letter.

She read it and gave a sharp cry. "It's from Geoffrey! My sister has been brought to bed a month before her time. The child is puny and Elizabeth is dreadfully ill. She wants me! Oh, I must go to her."

Verax stepped forward. "My dear, I am so sorry. Of course you must go. I will have the horses put to at once and I shall take you to your sister."

"There is no need for you to come."

He looked angry. "Naturally I shall accompany you. You forget she is my sister also now."

In her misery she lashed out at him. "Oh, naturally you will come with me! You would not relinquish your bride's bed so soon, would you?"

Fury blazed in his face, and she tried to draw back

as he seized her arm. "Is that what you think? You believe me to be so despicable!"

She tried to shake him off, but he grasped her more tightly until she almost cried out in pain. "Yes, you are despicable, but no more than any man. My sister's husband is good, yet he puts my dear Elizabeth through agony and danger over and over again. This illness is all his fault. He has no true affection, as I see it. All he has is lust!"

"And is that what I am supposed to feel for you?"

"What else? You do not care for me! You do not love me!"

"Do you dare to reproach me for that?"

"No! Why should I? But I expected chivalry, and you denied me even that."

"I have been tender with you, Cassandra. Many men would not have been."

"What are they to me?" She was filled with the memory of her sister, her figure gone, her looks ageing and the image mingled with her mother's. "What are *you* to me?" she half sobbed.

His voice cut through her turbulence and to her frantic mind his words were like a taunt. "For one night I thought I might mean much to you. Your first response to me . . ."

Anger and shame burnt her brain. She must stop him and, past knowing what she said, she heard her voice from the depth of her being as it revealed the terrors she had for years dammed behind a wall of cool sophistication. She spared him nothing. Her loathing and disgust were bared. She castigated men for holding women in callous disregard. She poured out words until none were left and he stared at her, his face white and disbelieving.

For a moment there was only the sound of a soft
spring wind rustling the leaves of the evergreens,
then Verax replied, "So! And I took you for a woman
of courage for holding fast to a belief in which she
had faith – the right of a woman to live alone if she
chose. I respected you for your valiant capitulation
when you accepted the necessity for marriage. But
truly, Cassandra, had I known the truth I would not
have wed you. Rather would I have left England for
ever!"

He held her at arm's length, looking her up and
down, his eyes bitter as they lingered on the curves of
her body. "The Crystal Venus," he murmured.
"How foolish of men to label you so, for you
have very pretty arms, have you not, my dear
wife?"

He slid his hands down to hers and bent and kissed
her arms. His lips retained the power to melt her
anger and when he released her suddenly she felt
dizzy.

He bowed. "I will escort you to your sister, but I
will not molest you again."

She watched as his tall figure strode away and her
eyes filled with wretched tears.

The journey over roads broken by heavy frost into
holes now filled with mud was concluded in two
days, and Cassandra forgot her problems to give
comfort to her sister. Elizabeth was pathetically glad
to see her and began to recover her health, encouraged daily by Cassandra's loving ministrations. The
baby thrived with his mother and Geoffrey was high
in his praise.

Lord and Lady Verax remained in Somerset for

six weeks and he kept his vow, sleeping in the small dressing-room attached to their bedchamber.

As the sisters said goodbye Elizabeth clung to Cassandra. "You are happy, aren't you, dearest? You do not seem well."

Cassandra assured her sister that only anxiety had affected her looks, but a suspicion of the truth kept her in a torment of suspense.

Back in Oxfordshire Verax suggested that they prepare for their interrupted journey to Paris, and she informed him that she wished to remain at Birkwood.

"As you please," he assented, apparently without interest, "though if you do not want to travel to Europe perhaps we could return to London. You would enjoy the celebrations. Lord Wellington has been made up into a duke and many hostesses are giving grand receptions for him; shall I escort you to town?"

Cassandra shook her head. "No, thank you, my lord. I prefer to remain here."

Verax looked angry. She was seated in her favourite place, a cushioned window-seat overlooking the timbered, grassy park which swept down to the river, where she could raise her eyes from her sewing or her book to watch passing craft, or the grazing deer.

"Will you spend the remainder of your days in the sulks? By God, madam, there are men who would not stand for such behaviour."

"I dare swear there are! Do you intend to join their ranks?"

He walked up and down the room twice, his long legs making short work of the small parlour. Then he stopped and stared down at her. She continued to sew, though her heart was beating hard. "Put down your needle," he ordered.

She laid her sewing aside. "Of what do you desire to talk?"

"Of Elizabeth! Of your mother and father! Of men and women in general!"

Revulsion coursed through her and she reached for her sewing, but he knocked it to the floor.

"You will spoil my stitching!"

"Damn your stitching! All you seem to think about is yourself, your own concerns, your own worries."

"You are incorrect, sir. I think of my sister."

"But in the wrong way. Elizabeth is a true woman – a creature full of love and tenderness, a wife of whom a man can be proud. Geoffrey loves her deeply."

"So deeply that he risks her life without thought."

"Oh, Cassandra, how mistaken you are! She adores her babies. She encourages his caresses. She must do, for a man as sensitive and full of care as Geoffrey would not force unwanted attentions upon her."

"Many men care nothing for losing a wife, or even two. My sister does her duty!"

Verax did not reply at once, then he sighed. "I cannot reach you."

"Then do not try. May I have my sewing, please?"

He picked it up and tossed it to her before he walked out of the room. They ate that night in almost total silence, and when she left the table he did not follow her. She felt unwell and could settle to nothing.

She heard Jonathan yelling for more wine. He must have consumed all that had been in the dining-room. She decided to go to bed, but could not sleep. Her mind revolved round her husband, downstairs, pouring wine into himself in an attempt to drown his frustration and disappointment. She stared into the darkness, fighting the knowledge that she missed the hard warmth of his body beside her; wishing she had never left Ridgefield one moment; the next longing to find enough courage to go down and tell him her news.

Once she heard him roar at Daniel, and knew that even his devoted servant was not allowed to watch over his master. When the house became silent she wondered if Jonathan was safe. She thought of the lighted candles and decided she must go to check on him.

Slowly she drew the bedcurtains and swung her legs to the floor. Before she could reach for her wrapper her door was flung open with a shattering bang and the Marquis stood on the threshold, a candle held so precariously that hot wax dripped on the carpet.

He swayed as he said thickly, "So, my adorable wife. You are ready for me."

Cassandra hung on to her composure. "I was coming to see if you needed help, my lord. Pray, go to your room and call your valet. You are drunk."

"Yes, my love, I am. Very drunk." He walked unsteadily towards her, then laying down the candle with exaggerated care he turned and slid his arms about her waist.

"Verax! You said . . .!"

"What a man vows in cold daylight he sometimes

forgets in wine-soaked night. What a stupid resolve
to make! I desire you . . . do you feel nothing for
me?" He brushed her hair with rough kisses. "No
matter! A man takes his pleasures without love, or
thought for the consequences, is not that so,
madam?"

"Apparently, my lord. Is that how you would take
me?"

He pushed her until the backs of her knees were
forced against the bed. She made no struggle.
Instead she spoke softly. "I am with child, sir."

All movement ceased. "What?"

"I am to bear your child."

The silence seemed to last for ever, and she
watched his face as the blurred features sharpened.
He released her and swept her a bow. "How very
unfortunate! My apologies, madam."

In a moment he was gone and Cassandra sank to
the bed, and tears which had been dammed for weeks
poured from her until she dropped into exhausted
sleep.

In the morning she felt sick and her head ached and
Eliza and Nurse came to frown over her, but she
refused their pleas to send for a physician. They went
into her boudoir and before they closed the door
Cassandra heard Nurse whisper to Eliza, "How was
you when you had your little one?"

She should have realised that her maids would
have recognised the signs, and the concern in
Nurse's voice touched her heart. It was the first time
she had admitted to believing Eliza's past history,
and it revealed the extent of her worry.

Cassandra wondered what Verax was doing. He

probably had a sore head and it served him right. How cruelly rough he had been. But why had she not told him before of the baby?

She answered her own question. Her wretched pride had once more impeded her. Having for so long clung to her much-vaunted independence she would not admit that, although nervous, her misconceptions had been swamped by the wonder of the new life she carried in her body. Might she also one day have found the courage to confess her love? His innate compassion would have filled him with tenderness. Perhaps time would have brought a renewal of his love for her. She was amazed by the change in herself. She seemed suddenly to be endowed with qualities of humble perception.

She vowed she would find a way to repair the damage she had wrought and she smiled and stretched, feeling better. "I will get up," she called, and Eliza dressed her in a cheerful flowered muslin gown.

Downstairs she sat in the window-seat, her book laid aside, her hands idle, waiting for Jonathan to come to her. But instead, Daniel brought a note which informed her briefly that her husband had gone to London. He reiterated his regret for what had occurred.

Cassandra was furious. How dared he go without seeing her? Then her new-born wisdom came to her aid. She had shamed her husband into absenting himself from a home which clearly he relished. Once before he had gone away from her and she had done nothing to stop him. She had known herself to be in the wrong, but pride had imprisoned her finer impulses. Years had been lost when they could have been happy together, and during those years she had created a barrier of myth around herself, deceiving herself and others because she had lost the only man she wanted. She had even consented to a "marriage of convenience", masking from herself her realisation that her surrender had been made easier by her love for him.

No more would she shrink from the consequences of her cowardice. She would display her love to him fearlessly, and give him a chance to respond.

She sped to her apartments, calling for Eliza. "A travelling gown and cloak. I am going to London!"

"But Miss . . . Lady Verax . . ." protested Eliza.

Nurse hobbled in. "You can't go gallivanting around, my lamb. You've only just had the long journey from Somerset. Stay here. His lordship will come round."

"Men are frequently transported on quite infantile impulses, especially after they have been inebriated," explained Eliza.

Nurse looked at her colleague with admiration. "That's true!" she declared, then paused reflectively. "At least, I think it is, though Eliza has the edge over me in learning."

Cassandra wondered if there was any area of life of which her maids were not fully conversant as she cried, "I am as strong as a horse, and I am going to London whether you accompany me or not."

"As if we wouldn't come!" said the scandalised servants.

Within the hour her ladyship's crested carriage was speeding along the London road in a manner which Nurse proclaimed disgraceful when her mistress was in an interesting condition. She sat grimly clutching the leather strap above her head while holding on to the large travelling medicine-chest she had insisted upon bringing, and even Eliza held hartshorn and a bottle of lavender water.

Cassandra could not brook delay. She must find Verax today, while the words she longed to say were bubbling on the surface of her mind. Tomorrow might be too late. Tomorrow she might capitulate to craven fear of her husband's reaction.

They had covered about fifteen miles and were travelling fast along a part of the road narrowed by cartwheel-rutted sides when her coachman and grooms began to yell. The coach swayed and Cassandra looked from the window in time to see a phaeton and four matching bay horses, handled with masterly control, sweep past them with inches to spare. She recognised the driver as he saw her.

The phaeton was dragged to a halt and Cassandra shrieked to her coachman to stop. A moment later Verax was opening the carriage door and helping his wife down the steps.

Wordlessly they abandoned their vehicles, oblivious of the fury of several following travellers, and the Marquis led his wife to a small path leading into a wood. Out of sight of the others they stopped and looked at one another.

"I was returning to you," said Verax.

"I was coming after you," said Cassandra.

Blue eyes and brown locked in a battle for supremacy which neither won. Verax held out his arm and Cassandra laid her fingers upon it, and they walked beside the river.

"I owe you an apology for my behaviour of last night," Verax said a little stiffly.

Cassandra bent her head in acknowledgement. "You are generous, sir. I am your wife – I have not the . . . the right to deny you."

Verax faltered in his stride and Cassandra reminded him quickly, "I was about to come downstairs to see that you came to no harm."

"Then you care about me – perhaps a little, Cassandra?"

A little! cried her heart. *I love you, my darling.* Cassandra swallowed hard, before she said, "Did . . . did you truly love Susan?"

He stopped and turned her face to his. "Look at me and tell me that you ever believed I would fall victim to the charms of such an addlepate!"

Cassandra smiled. "I have observed men make utter idiots of themselves over entirely unsuitable girls."

"Indeed! Pray, do not count me among their number!"

He replaced her hand upon his arm and they resumed walking. "I made an idiot of myself over one woman only in my life, and you well know who she was."

Cassandra's heart beat uncomfortably fast. "You did not think you were foolish at the time," she said in a small voice.

Again he stopped, and this time she could not meet his eyes. Slowly he took her chin in a firm grasp and tilted her face to his. "Look at me, Cassandra!"

She kept her lids lowered, but her heart was now racing as fast as her thoughts. Was there tenderness in his voice? Was there something more?

She raised her lids and looked deep into his dark eyes. He bent his head and kissed her lips with infinite tenderness. He was breathing hard and his eyes expressed his desire. "I love you, Cassandra. In the past, present – and always. Could you not guess?"

She shook her head. "I did not dare to hope."

"Hope? You wanted my love?"

"So very much! I know it now. It was always so. Oh, what a weakling I have been! And when you, my husband, gave me the chance to redeem myself, I would not take it. No wonder men called me . . . called me . . . 'The Crystal Venus'."

"Insolent dogs," said Verax, laughter sharpening his voice. "Fools also! But I am glad you held yourself so cool and aloof from other men. I dreamed of my hands being the ones to unlock your ice-bound prison and reveal your true nature to us both. And that first night – I was sure from the way you responded. . . ."

She blushed and shivered with delight at her memories as she murmured, "All the wasted years. All my fault!"

"Oh, no! Mine too. I left England. I ran away from you because I could not face further humiliation and disappointment."

"I could have acted quickly to hold you here. I was proud, foolish and cowardly."

She felt his sudden tension. "Cowardly? Cassandra, you must be honest with me. Did you mean all those terrible things you said about marriage and children?"

"I meant them at the time. I have thought them, or I believed I did. Oh, Jonathan, I scarcely know what I felt! After years of thinking myself so untouchable I found myself helpless in the grip of . . ."

"Of what, my dear?"

She took a deep breath. "Of love, my darling husband."

He slid his arms about her and his lips caressed her face. "I never thought to hear those words from you. I have suffered such agonies of longing. Say what I need to hear. Say it quickly."

"I love you, Jonathan," said Cassandra, and having begun to unlock her heart and her tongue she found she knew the language of tenderness and passion.

His arms tightened about her. They stood so close she felt she had become a part of him. His mouth became searching and demanding so that her will was lost in his, and she responded with a hunger all the more abandoned for having been suppressed.

At last he raised his head. "My dearest love! What joy we shall know! And, Cassandra, you are not angry with me – or fearful of bearing our child?"

Cassandra laughed. "Of course I am a little fearful – what woman would not be? – at any rate, the first time. But I look forward with great longing to holding our baby."

His kisses became even more satisfactory and they wandered back along the river bank, pausing often to utter words of love and exchange caresses and endearments in the sweet scents of a June forest, until they arrived back on the highway.

Lord and Lady Verax's grooms were doing their utmost to excuse the fact that two coaches blocked the passage of anything on wheels. Nurse was bandying insults with an equally elderly maid and Eliza was wringing her hands in horror at her lack of gentility.

As the Marquis tenderly assisted his wife up a

slight rise to the road an irate gentleman with a corpulent figure and a red face saw him and shouted, "Are you responsible for this disgraceful hold-up?"

Verax swept him a bow. "I fear I am, sir. Pray accept my apologies," he called to everyone within earshot.

"I would not have believed it possible for so much chaos to occur in so short a time," he murmured to a wife who had been seized by a fit of helpless giggling. The corpulent gentleman looked in danger of bursting, and a lady in a large green bonnet added her reproaches from the window of her carriage. Cassandra implored her husband to restore order.

"I will do anything for you, my love," he responded. He handed Cassandra into his phaeton where he lingered lovingly to tuck a lap-robe about her, to the increased fury of the old gentleman. Then he ordered his groom to join her ladyship's servants in the large travelling-carriage and proceed with it to a point at which it could turn.

With consummate skill he manoeuvred his horses and the elegant phaeton past the queue of coaches, bowing and raising his long whip in salute to the outraged travellers who stared at them while Cassandra tried to control her mirth.

The horses gained speed and they began to leave the others behind. The Marquis looked down at his wife, whose lips still curved in a smile. "Are you truly pleased about the baby?"

"Delighted," said Cassandra dreamily.

"And you will not mind all the inconveniences? The crying in which a baby indulges; the inconsistencies in its behaviour?"

She looked up and he smiled apologetically.

"Between battles I visited fellow officers and their families. That is how I know these things."

"I shall not mind any of it," promised Cassandra.

"Not even sticky lips and fingers, and the propensity for sudden dampness and that kind of thing?"

Cassandra was silent for a moment. "I know there are excellent nursemaids to be had – and of course my own dear Nurse will supervise all the arrangements. We can trust her, Jonathan, and you will not require me to give too much of my time to our children?"

He bent to plant a kiss on the crown of her stylish blue silk hat. "On the contrary! I shall expect you to devote yourself to me!"

Cassandra leaned against him contentedly. The future might hold disagreements and the occasional argument. They had been independent too long to yield readily. But there would be days of sharing, nights of joy. They would have a lifetime of learning to know one another.

Today she was happy to drive with him in the June sun, to relax in the bliss and comfort of her husband's strength and the surety of his love.

Masquerade
Historical Romances

Intrigue excitement romance

Don't miss
June's
other enthralling Historical Romance title

SATAN'S MOUNTAIN
by Kate Buchan

Miss Helen Shaw of Boston, New England, is delighted to learn she has become an heiress. The inheritance of her grandfather's house in the Connecticut mountains, together with a half-share in his prosperous ironworks nearby, means he has finally forgiven her mother's impetuous runaway marriage. She sets out to claim her new property, only to find that even in the enlightened days following the American Civil War, sinister superstitions still linger amongst the mountain folk. For they call St. Thomas's Mountain — site of the ironworks — Satan's Mountain ... because they believe that Helen's cousin and fellow-heir, Robert Warren, is in league with the devil. And how can Helen disagree with this belief when the saturnine Robert is clearly determined to be her implacable enemy?

You can obtain this title today from your local paperback retailer

Doctor Nurse Romances

and June's
stories of romantic relationships behind the scenes
of modern medical life are:

STAFF NURSE AT ST. MILDRED'S
Janet Ferguson

Staff Nurse Jill Thompson was not used to feeling
unsure of herself. She liked things to be well organised,
like her future with Clive Farmer. But perhaps she was
only clinging to Clive because Dr Guy Ferring, her boss
at St. Mildred's, disturbed her so . . .

THE RUSTLE OF BAMBOO
Celine Conway

Inexperienced as she was, Nurse Pat Millay found it
hard going at the little hospital on the Burmese island
of Pelonga. And that was before she had experienced
the abrasive effect of Dr Mark Bradlaw's personality —
or fallen in love with him . . .

Order your copies today from your local paperback retailer

Masquerade
Historical Romances

**Intrigue
excitement
romance**

COUNT ANTONOV'S HEIR
by Christina Laffeaty

To Caroline Kearley, fresh from England, Imperial
Russia was a bewildering place where magnificence
and privilege existed side by side with poverty and
degradation. And she held a secret that could strip
Count Alexander Antonov — whom she loved more
than her own happiness — of his wealth and power
overnight!

CAPTAIN BLACK
by Caroline Martin

Wealthy Puritan heiress Deborah Halsey was kidnapped
so that her ransom could swell the Royalist coffers —
and to strike a blow at Sir Edward Biddulph, her
betrothed. The man who captured her was Sir
Edward's mortal enemy — so why should Deborah
feel so happy as prisoner of the notorious Captain
Black?

Look out for these titles in your local paperback shop from
11th July 1980

Masquerade
Historical Romances

Intrigue excitement romance

FOLLOW THE DRUM
by Judy Turner

To escape an arranged marriage, Barbara Campion
fled from home determined to find her soldier sweet-
heart. Daringly disguised as a boy, she enlisted in the
Rifle Brigade and followed the drum through Belgium
to the Battle of Waterloo — under the command of
the fascinating Captain Alleyn . . .

STOLEN INHERITANCE
by Anne Madden

Deborah Wyngarde's journey to London with her
brother Philip, to claim their inheritance from the
newly-restored King Charles II, seemed wasted when
they were scorned as impostors. And Deborah had
meanwhile lost her heart to the Earl of Mulgarth —
whom even his sister declared to be a hardened rake!

These titles are still available through your local paperback
retailer